NOAH'S NAVY

Dream Doors Adventures Book 2

DOUGLAS HIRT
TERRY JAMES

Noah's Navy
Dream Doors Adventures Book 2
Douglas Hirt
Terry James

CKN Christian Publishing
An Imprint of Wolfpack Publishing
6032 Wheat Penny Avenue
Las Vegas, NV 89122

ISBN: 978-1-64119-169-2

NOAH'S NAVY

On the joyous day that Adam Beam and his sister Zonia returned the stolen sack of apples to the Great King, a fabulous celebration filled the golden streets of Glorainia. Thousands of New Edenites gathered in the parks and avenues to give praise to the Great King, and high honors to the two children and their magnificent Siberian Tiger named Toby who had served the King so valiantly.

On that day The Great King revealed to Adam Beam the special task that he and Zonia were to undertake next. The apples, carried out of the Garden of Eden thousands of years earlier by the Grandfather Adam and Grandmother Eve, would be planted throughout the land of New Eden. Their fruit would become a blessing to the people, as it had been the First Time. All things were being made new again.

Everyone was very pleased that Adam and

Zonia would be serving the Great King in this new venture . . . well, almost everyone.

Even now, during New Eden time where there was much goodness and happiness, evil still lurked in the hearts of some New Edons.

Two such New Edons watched the celebration with envy in their hearts. Short and heavy, seventeen-year-old Lester Mudd scowled as he heard the Great King's proclamation. He wished it was he himself receiving Adam's praise. When the crowds raised a shout of joy for Adam Beam, Lester Mudd snarled and ground his teeth together. He wanted that joy to be his, and his alone.

Standing at Lester's side, the taller, lankier Castor Groutt wore an unhappy frown too. "W-why is everyone making such a fuss, Lester? They didn't do nothing so great."

Lester Mudd looked at Castor Groutt with squinty eyes full of mischief. He was already working on a dark plot. If there was to be a reward and honor, it was going to be his own and not those two little kids. "I heard that he stole those apples from the Evols. That was wrong."

"B-but the Great King didn't punish him. He rewarded him, and his kid sister."

Lester hardly heard Castor. His brain was busy working out the details of his evil plan. "Those apples must be pretty important to the Evols. Those Evols would probably pay me a big reward to get them back."

"H-how we going to get them apples back to the Evols, Lester?"

Lester whacked Castor on the head with his ball cap. "You bonehead."

"Hey! W-why'd you do that, Lester?" Castor rubbed the top of his head.

"How do you think we're going to do it? We'll steal the apples from the Adam Beam kid and then Dream Doodle ourselves back to the First Time."

Castor looked confused. "B-but we don't have a Dream Doodler, Lester. An-and I flunked Dream Doodling when I was in Exploretime.

Lester rolled his eyes. "Nobody flunks Dream Doodling, bonehead."

"Well, I almost flunked," Castor corrected. "I was supposed to Dream Doodle back to the time of Blackbeard the pirate but I landed on the deck of a boat fishing for sardines two hundred years later."

Lester rolled his eyes again. "I'll do the Dream Doodling. You can carry the sack of apples."

Castor's face brightened. "O-okay. That sounds easy." But we still don't have a Dream Doodler," he said, confused.

Lester whipped off his hat again. Castor flinched and covered his head. Lester snarled and tugged the hat back on his head. "Tonight we'll get a Dream Doodler. Just keep your mouth shut and do what I tell you and everything will work out. We'll steal the apples from the Beam kid and then

Dream Doodle us back to the First Time . . . and a great big reward!"

* * *

ADAM BEAM COULD HARDLY CONTAIN his excitement the rest of the day. Not only had he served the Great King, but the King had entrusted him and Zonia with yet another important job, and another way to serve. Zonia was excited too.

Even Toby knew something grand had happened. The huge Siberian Tiger romped around the house like a kitten, giving Adam and Zonia tigerback rides up and down the stairs. Bud Beam, Adam's father, tossed the giant cat three ripe red fruiton treats and then a big bowl full of catvage from the manna manger. Toby had been as much a part of the *Adam's Apples* adventures as his children had been.

Molly Beam, Adam's mother, was going to cook a special dinner for the family. No manna manger food tonight, although the manna manger always gave them delicious meals whenever they wanted them. No, tonight Molly Beam was going to prepare family dinner just the way she remembered her own mother cooking Sunday dinners in the Before Time.

When the family gathered around the dinner table, Adam's father led them in a prayer to the Great King and the King's Father thanking them for the opportunity to serve them, also for the wonderful food prepared by Molly's hands, and finally for the amazing task the Great King had give to Adam and Zonia. It was always exciting when a New Edonite was able to serve the Great King in a special way.

Afterward, everyone was too excited to go to bed, so Molly Beam read aloud a story about Children in the Before Time.

Adam had a hard time understanding the troubles Before Time children faced. Mrs. Beam explained that in the Before Time, the Serpent was free to torment people, but in New Eden times, the evil serpent was locked away in a prison where he couldn't harm children or grownups.

"I'm glad he can't hurt us now," Zonia said with a rush of relief.

Toby seemed to understand her, and he gave a deep growl of agreement.

Adam thought about that for a moment. "But there are still people doing bad things?" He remembered a few weeks earlier when a farmer's market peddler was caught using a scale that weighed flour too heavy so that people who bought from him were paying too many trade coins.

Molly Beam looked sad. "That's because we are still human. That poor peddler still suffers from Grandfather Adam's disobedience, way back in the First Time. You remember how sad he looked when he spoke to you about it, don't you?"

Adam and Zonia nodded. It had only been two days since he'd left Grandfather Adam and brought the sack of apples back to New Eden Time.

"I remember," Adam said in a heavy voice, and then his face lit up with a big smile. "But someday we'll be like the Brightons, and never do bad things ever again."

Bud Beam grinned and put a hand on Adam's shoulder. "Yes, someday our old nature will be gone and we'll be Brightons. Until then, he must try hard to do what we know the Great King would want us to do."

That night Adam lay in bed thinking about what his mom and dad had said, and about the job the Great King had given him to do. He looked at the sack of precious apples on the table in the corner of his bedroom. He was anxious to begin planting the seeds they contain.

Laying there under the light sheet, he sent off a prayer to the Great King, and immediately felt sleepy-eyed. He looked at the sack of apples again, and around his cozy room seeing the dark pictures on the wall. The last thing he remembered was the big wooden model of Noah's Ark on the shelf by the door that his dad had helped him build.

And then he was asleep.

And then suddenly something woke him up!

* * *

LESTER MUDD TIPTOED in the darkness, creeping along the hallway that led to the Exploretime cube. He'd thought to bring a flashlight with him, but now he was afraid to turn it on. He didn't want the light to be seen past the large windows that over-looked all of Glorainia.

He stopped suddenly when he heard a noise from one of the dark classrooms. Castor Groutt crashed into his back, nearly knocking him down.

"You bonehead!" Lester hissed slapping Castor atop his head with his ball cap.

"H-hey. Whydya do that for, Lester?"

Lester tugged the ball cap back on his head so hard his ears stuck out like a hippopotamus. "Shut up. You want us to get caught?" Lester listened, but the noise had stopped. The boys resumed creeping along the dark wall. They fumbled in the darkness when they reached the Exploretime storage room just behind the Exploretime cube.

Castor tumbled over a chair and fell onto one of the student work tables. Another chair crashed onto its side and a container of pencils clattered to the floor and rolled round and round.

"Bonehead!" Lester hissed and popped his partner in crime on the head again with the flashlight."

"Ouch!"

"Watch where you step, bonehead. You're gonna get us caught. We'll be in big trouble if the Lighton finds us here."

7

Castor shivered at the thought of a huge Lighton appearing out of nowhere and hauling them off to the district Brighton. "M-Maybe we oughta leave, Lester," he said worriedly, looking over his shoulder out the window at the twinkling lights of Gloriania.

"Just be quiet and we'll be okay," Lester whispered. "Here, I found the cabinet where the Dream Doodlers are kept — at least this is where they *use* to keep them when I was here." He opened the cabinet door and felt around in the dark cabinet. "Ah! Here they are, just like remembered." He lifted out a Dream Doodler. "Now let's get outta here."

Castor Grout fumbled through the cabinet making more noise.

"I said, let's go! What's wrong with you, bonehead? Don't you understand New Edonish?"

"W-we need a Dream Doodler holster too. The two work together."

Lester had forgotten that part. "Oh. Yeah, you're right. Hey, I thought you said you flunked Dream Doodling?"

"Almost flunked," Castor said, irritated. "Here it is." He yanked the belt out of the cabinet, spilling two more Dream Doodlers on the floor with a loud clatter.

"Bonehead!" Lester grabbed Castor by the shirt and pulled him into the dark hallway and out the door where they stood in the shadows of the building, listening.

But the night remained quiet except for the soft chirping of crickets.

"Whew. We're in the clear now," Lester said.

Castor and Lester walked along the dark path between tall trees that led away from the Explore-time building. Castor said, "T-tell me again, Lester. What's your plan?"

Lester looked at Castor with disgust. "I've told you a hundred times now," he said with exasperation in his voice. "We're gonna take this here Dream Doodler and with it we're gonna dream draw the sack of apples into our hands. Then we dream doodle ourselves and them apples backwards in time to the First Time where they came from. Those Evol people will be so happy to get the apples back that they'll give us a reward. Maybe gold or something. They had lots of gold back then."

Castor wondered why Lester wanted gold when even the streets of Glorainia were paved with the stuff? But he didn't mention that to his partner in crime because Lester was smarter than he was. And he didn't want to get whacked on the head again.

Chapter 2

LESTER AND CASTOR SKULKED DOWN THE STEEP stairway into the dark basement that the two boys used for their hideout; a shadowy place that smelled of wet cardboard and moldy food. It hadn't been cleaned for months. Lester and Castor preferred it that way.

Lester pulled a chain and turned on the single light bulb that dangled from the ceiling. With a *swoosh* of his arm he swept away the remains of yesterday's lunch from the cluttered, wobbly table. He opened the brown paper bag they had carried with them since leaving the Exploretime building.

Castor reached for the Dream Doodler.

Lester smacked his hand with the flashlight.

"*Oww!* Hey, why'd you do that?" Castor whined, rubbing his hand.

"You ain't got no business fooling with that

Doodler. You flunked Dream Doodling, remember?"

"I said I *almost* flunked."

Lester ignored him and picked up the Dream Doodler. "Looks just the way I remember it," he said holding it toward the light bulb. "See? Here's the green button that you push when you want to draw a dream picture."

"I know. Le-Lemme see it." Castor grabbed for the Dream Doodler.

Lester moved it out of his reach. "Don't touch. Just observe. I ain't taking no chances with a amateur pushin' the wrong button. Now, this button here makes you whatchamacallit, you know, disappear."

"It's called the Disappear Dazzler button," Castor said. "I-I remember it from Dream Doodling class.

"Yeah, I knew that," Lester said grouchily. He pressed the button and disappeared.

Startled, Castor stumbled backward and fell over a stack of old paint cans spilling red and yellow paint across their dingy concrete floor.

A second later Lester reappeared, laughing at Castor. "Scared ya didn't I?"

"That wasn't nice." Castor got up off the floor and shook off the globs of paint soaking his shirt sleeve.

Lester looked at the Dream Doodler with a mischievous glee in his eyes. "We can do lots of quantum stuff with this gadget. For starts, we're gonna get us some apples."

Castor tried to touch it again.

Lester whacked his head. "Don't touch nothin', bonehead. Anybody who flunked Dream Doodling has no business fooling around with a Dream Doodler."

"I didn't flunk!" Castor said with irritation in his voice. "I *ALMOST* flunked,"

"Shut up. We got business to take care of." Lester squinted as he thought about what they were going to do next. "What we gotta do now is get to that kid's house — what's his name?"

"Adam Beam."

"Yeah, yeah. I remember."

"Yo-you know where he lives?" Castor asked.

"We don't have to know where he lives, bone-head. This here Dream Doodler will find his house for us. Don't you know nothin'? No wonder you flunked Dream Doodling."

"*I . . . DIDN'T . . . FLUNK!*"

"All I got to do is think about those apples, and that kid, and wave the Dream Doodler like this and push the Dream Draw button and . . ."

A dream door suddenly appeared in the middle of the hideout. It was black as ink, and Castor couldn't see a single thing in it. "It's aw-awful dark, Lester."

"Bonehead! You don't think I'd be so stupid as to dream draw us someplace where we'd be seen, do you? Come on, jump into this thing before it closes." Lester grabbed Castor's arm, getting red paint on his fingers, and together they jumped through the dream door portal.

They landed in the dark, stumbled, and tumbled to the floor.

"Now look what you done!" Lester whacked his partner on the head.

"It wasn't my dream doodle," Castor whined.

"*Ssshh!* You wanna get us caught?" Lester got carefully to his feet.

"Wh-where are we?" Castor said feeling soft things hanging down all around them. "You dream doodled us into a closet."

"Keep your voice down, bonehead." Lester found the door knob and quietly opened the door and looked around. "This here is the kid's bedroom."

Lester and Castor poked their heads out the door. Soft moonlight came through the window, falling upon the foot of the bed where Adam Beam slept. The pale moon glow crawled up the wall and shown upon a shelf where some of the boy's toys were neatly arranged. Castor cringed. He liked his stuff messy.

Amongst the toys was the model of a huge boat with rows of toy animals lined up to enter through a big door on the side.

"Hey, Lester. Look. There's Noah's Ark."

Lester whacked Castor across the head with his

cap. "Stop looking at the toys and keep your voice down. We've got to find that sack of apples."

"Okay. Ya d-don't have to hit me all the time."

The two boys crept quietly from the closet. Lester halted and listened. The only sound in the room was Adam Beam's soft breathing. They tiptoed around the foot of Adam's bed. Castor stopped to look at all the animals lined up on the shelf, marching like in a parade into the big, wooden ark. He thought it would have been fun to have sailed with Noah. Then he remembered how that world had become so evil, and that God had to send a huge flood to kill all the wicked people. Only Noah and his family survived. Suddenly Castor wasn't so sure sailing with Noah would have been fun after all.

"There," Lester whispered, pointing at a table in the shadowy corner of the bedroom. Silent as a mouse, Lester tiptoed to the sack.

Castor spied a long-necked apatosaurus among the toy animals and decided he wanted it. But when he reached for it, he bumped the other miniature animals and they all came clattering to the floor.

Startled, Lester spun about, knocking over a lamp on the night stand. It crashed loudly.

Adam Beam sat straight up and rubbed the sleep from his eyes. "Who are you?"

Lester scrambled back, but his feet slipped out from under him because of all the toy animals on the floor. He and Castor crashed to the floor too. The Dream Doodler went flying.

"What are you doing in my bedroom?" Adam asked, more surprised than frightened.

Outside the door, a fearsome roar shook the room and the door trembled when Toby put his paws against it.

"Let's get out of here!" Lester shouted.

Castor sat up and his hand fell upon the Dream Doodler.

Lester was trying to get up, but he was having trouble.

Adam Beam said, "You're not suppose to be here." He was still in shock. No one in Gloriania ever entered other people's homes without being invited, and he was pretty sure he didn't know who these two strangers in his bedroom were. It was a sure thing they hadn't been invited.

"Use the Dream Doodler," Lester cried, finally getting to his knees.

Castor couldn't think of anyplace to dream doodle them to. His brain was confused and not working quickly — it never worked quickly even when it wasn't confused. He glanced about the dark bedroom, his view stumbled across the wooden model of Noah's Ark. He closed his eyes, pressed the green dream draw button and waved the dream doodler in the air.

Instantly a dream door portal opened in the Adam's bedroom. The scene it showed was gloomy.

Thunder rumbled and lightening flashed. In their panic to escape, neither Castor nor Lester much cared what the drawing was showing them. Both boys leaped through the portal, and it closed behind them.

* * *

TOBY PROWLED around Adam's bedroom sniffing the floor. When he poked his head into the closet, he gave a low growl.

Adam's dad and mom, both wrapped in their robes, looked around the room and then at Adam, sitting on the edge of his bed. "They made a mess of your room," Molly Beam said.

Adam shivered. "Why did they come here?" In the bright light from the lamp that they picked up and had turned on, he didn't feel quite so scared.

Bud Beam shook his head. "If this had been the Before Time, I'd have guessed they were burglars. But now we're in New Eden time and burglars are not a problem today."

"What are burglars?" Zonia asked. She wore a pink fuzzy robe, and her feet were bare. When Toby had roared, he had awoken them all and none had time to find their slippers.

Bud Beam sighed, his voice sounding sad. "In the Before Time, bad men would break into people's houses at night to steal stuff." He shook his head. "I thought we'd left that all behind when the

Great King came to earth to rule New Eden from this throne in Gloriania. I keep forgetting that we are still children of Adam, still sinners, even though few of us really want to disobey the Great King."

"That's kind of scary," Zonia said. "Did the burglars steal anything from your room, Adam?"

Adam hadn't even thought about that. Stealing things was just not something people did in New Eden. He looked around. "I don't think so . . ." His view landed upon the empty table in the corner and his eyes suddenly got large. "Adam's Apples! They were right there when I went to sleep. Now they're gone!"

"Oh no," Zonia cried and tears shined in her eyes. Toby snarled a very upset snarl.

Adam stared at his parents in disbelief, and he felt like he wanted to cry too.

"Now, now, Sunbeam," Mr. Beam said hugging Zonia tightly and kissing her cheek. "We'll get the apples back, don't worry. Those two boys won't get away with stealing them."

Mrs. Beam looked worried. "How can something like this happen? It's the sort of thing we feared in the Before Time, when I was a little girl."

Zonia sniffed and bravely choked back her tears. "But the Great King will be so disappointed."

Molly Beam hugged Zonia too. "The Great King knows how hard you two worked to save the apples. He knows this isn't your fault."

Adam slipped off his bed and planted his hands

on his waist. "We're going to have to get those apples back, that's all there is to it."

Toby growled and tossed his head in agreement.

"First thing we've got to do is figure out where they've taken the apples." Adam spied something in the corner and went to investigate closer.

"How are you going to do that?" Adam's dad asked?

"With this!" He picked up the Dream Doodler holster the thieves had dropped.

Bud looked at Molly. Neither knew what Adam had in mind, but Zonia did.

"The replay button on the Dream Doodler," she said, wiping the tears from her eyes.

"But you don't have the Dream Doodler, honey," Molly Beam pointed out. The thieves have it.

"Not for long," Adam said with a grin as he unbuckled the holster around his waist.

Chapter 3

LESTER AND CASTOR TUMBLED THROUGH THE stormy air and landed hard on a surface. It was a wooden surface like the deck of a boat and it leaped and bucked, pitched and yawed beneath them in wild gyrations tossing Lester and Castor this way and that. And if that wasn't bad enough, giant waves of warm water crashed across the deck, soaking them while icy rain hammered down on them.

"Whoooo! I'm slipping," Lester cried, rolling this way and that.

Castor, being taller and lankier and not so inclined to rolling as his roly-poly partner in crime, dropped the Dream Doodler and grabbed Lester with one hand. His other hand held onto an upright piece of wood that luckily had come into his gripping fingers.

"Where are we?" Castor cried!

Lester was too busy coughing up water to answer. Another big, drowning wave pounded over him and swept the sack of apples out of his fingers. Both the apples and the Dream Doodler plunged it into the violent waves and disappeared. But that was the least of the two thieves worry.

Lester blinked water from his eyes and tried to look around. He was barely able to see beyond the wooden deck of what suddenly he realized was a boat. A BIG boat!

"You bonehead!" Lester screamed as thunder pounded his ears and lightening nearly blinded him. "You dream doodled us onto Noah's Ark! Quick, dream draw us out of here!"

"I-I can't Lester. I lost the Dream Doodler!"

"Bonehead!"

Through the roaring storm, Lester spied a glimpse of light just past the piece of wood that Castor was holding onto for dear life. "There's a window!" he shouted.

Castor craned his neck. "Y-you're right, Lester."

Together the two bungling thieves clawed their way to the window and tumbled through it.

Oooomp! They landed on something kind of hard and kind of soft, but at least they were out of the storm. Lester sat up and looked around. The window above them was one of many that ran most of the length of the huge boat as far as he could see. The far distance was shrouded in gloom.

Flashes of lightening momentarily giving him glimpses of the immense size of the place.

"Dirt?" Castor said, scooping up a handful of the stuff where he sat.

Lester plucked up a crushed tomato plant from beneath him. "This must be where Noah grows his food." They'd landed on a high, shadowy ledge. Softly glowing lights showed a cluttered deck about ten feet lower. The middle of that deck was open and Lester could see down to another below that one. The light down there was even dimmer.

Castor sniffed. "What's that smell?"

"Animals, bonehead. Noah's Ark was a floating zoo. Don't you remember anything from your Exploretime lessons?"

The sound of footsteps reached them over the crashing thunder outside. "Oh-oh." Lester lowered his voice. "Someone must have heard us." A beam of light flashed across the ceiling.

Lester and Castor scrambled off the planting beds and scurried down the catwalk into the far shadows where the long row of windows ended. They crunched into a dark corner and peeked around it.

Two men came up a staircase and stood upon the catwalk looking around. The older of the two held something like a flashlight, only it appeared to be flat against his palm as he shined it along the planting beds.

"I was sure we heard it, father," the younger

man said. He wore something that looked like a bandage wrapped round and round his head.

"I believe you, Shem, but there can be nobody here. We eight are the only people on board."

They were dressed strangely in dark coats with tall collars, and baggy pants tucked into the tops of tall boots.

Shem scratched his head. "Maybe it's those monkeys again. You know how clever they are. The female has figured out how to undo the latch to their cage."

"Maybe." The older man shook his head, took another look around and was about to leave when something caught his eye. He turned back, bent over the planting bed and picked something up. In a flash of lightening from outside Lester saw that it was the tomato plant he had crushed.

"Look at this." The older man held the plant in the glow of his palm light. "Ripped right out of the garden. I think you're right, Shem. Let's see if we can find those mischievous monkeys."

When they left, Lester and Castor crawled out of their hiding place.

Castor said, "That must have been Noah."

"It was. I remember seeing pictures of him in Exploretime."

"Oh-oh yeah, I remember too."

Lester hit him over the head with his cap. "No you don't, bonehead. You're just saying that."

"Ouch."

"Keep you're voice down and let's figure a way out of here before we get caught. If only you hadn't lost the Dream Doodler."

"It wasn't my fault. Anyway, you lost the apples."

Lester scowled but he looked away without arguing. Castor was right, and he hated it whenever that happened.

The two boys sat in the dark with lightening casting weird shadows all around. The Ark lurched this way and that upon the powerful waves that tossed the boat. Frightening thunder pounded their ears.

Castor put his hands on his stomach. "I don't feel too good, Lester."

"Don't get seasick now. Noah will find us for sure if you do. Let's look around."

They crept along the narrow catwalk-like floor to the stairs at the other end and looked down onto the main floor. Nearby cages held small animals — too many for Lester to count. Beyond the cages the light became brighter. A little way aways a big door opened into a room where Lester glimpsed people moving around. It looked like dinner was being served on a long table.

Lester's stomach gave a hunger grumble. "Food."

"Ugh." Castor looked pale, kind of bent over and holding his stomach.

"Maybe we can get our hands on some of that food. Come on, and be quiet!"

Lester started down the stairs, trying to step softly. But the stairs squeaked with each step. Luckily, the thunder and the creaking of the ark rolling in the waves were louder. On the main floor he stopped and listened. He didn't hear anything but the thunder outside, so he crept toward the light where the people were.

SWOOOSH! Something swept through the air and came down over his head. He cried out in fright and tried to escape the thing, but his arms were pinned tightly to his side.

SWOOOSH! Something swept through the air and came down on Castor.

The *somethings* were round nets on the end of a long pole. Holding the two poles were Noah and Shem. Noah looked at his son and gave a low, soft laugh. "We found those monkeys."

Shem chuckled. "Looks like we got us a couple of stowaways."

Lester and Castor fought to free themselves from the nets, but it was no use. They'd been caught!

* * *

"OUR DREAM DOORS LIGHTON, Zekor, told us about this secret button," Adam explained, showing his mom and dad the tiny shiny button hidden beneath the holster's buckle.

"That's right," Zonia added. "We used it to get the Dream Doodler back from those awful Evols when we were lost inside the cave with Enoch."

Molly Beam glanced at Bud Beam. She looked worried. "I didn't know Dream Door adventures could be so dangerous."

"Nothing bad can happen to you in a Dream Door adventure," Zonia said confidently, repeating what Zekor had told them many times.

Adam's dad appeared more curious than worried. "How does it work?" He asked.

Adam said, "You just press the button like this."

WHOOMP! In an instant the Dream Doodler appeared in the holster. It was dripping wet with bits of green seaweed clinging to the handle.

"OH!" Molly Beam said, startled. "My, how clever."

"And convenient," Adam's dad added.

Zonia ran to the bathroom and returned with a towel to dry it off. Toby sniffed at the puddle of water on the floor the dripping Dream Doodle had made. Zonia cleaned that up too.

"Now we can see where the thieves went," Adam said.

"Where ever it was," their mother said, "it must be a very wet place."

Adam turned the Dream Doodler over and

twisted a switch recessed in the bottom of its handle.

"What does that do, honey?" his mom asked.

"That's the replay switch," Zonia said. "Mrs. Levin used it to show everyone's Dream Draw Adventure. That's part of what we learn in Exploretime."

Adam said, "It must put the Dream Doodler in reverse because now when I push the DREAM DRAW button, it draws a picture of where it's been, not where it's going."

Mr. Beam said, "I think we ought to invite Adam's Exploretime Lighton to see this too. After all, he's in charge of the Exploretime Cube and Dream Drawing."

"Good idea, dad," Zonia said. "Can I call him?"

"Sure, sweetheart."

Zonia stood very straight and closed her eyes in concentration, thinking the words instead of speaking them out loud. *To Adam's Dream Doors Lighton. Can you come right away? The Great King's apples have been stolen again-!, and we want to rescue them . . . again.*

Almost at once Zekor answered her inside her head. *Of course, Zonia. I'll be right there.*

She opened her eyes and looked at her mom. "He's on his wa-"

Adam's bedroom filled with bright colors that swirled round and round. With a brilliant flash,

Zekor the Lighton appeared in the room, bent over so that his head didn't hit the ceiling.

He smiled and the children ran to him. Zekor knelt on the floor and gave them a big hug. The children almost disappeared in the Lighton's huge arms. "I'm excited to see the two of you again," he said, his voice deep and powerful, yet gentle and loving.

Adam said, "Two thieves stole Adam's Apples."

Zonia said, "The Great King will be so disappointed."

"Don't be sad, little one." He gave Zonia another hug. "The Great King will never be disappointed with either you or Adam. In fact, he already knows all about the theft."

"He does?" Zonia's eyes widened.

Adam said, "The Great King knows everything."

"Yes indeed, He does," Zekor said. "And he knows that you and your sister, and Toby are just the right three to get Adam's Apples back."

"We are?" Now it was Adam's turn to be surprised.

Bud Beam said, "It sounds like another Dream Door Adventure for the three of you."

"Will it be dangerous?" Molly Beam asked.

"Nothing can hurt you in a Dream Door adventure," Adam, Zonia, and Zekor said at the same time.

Zonia said excitedly, "Push the replay button. I

want to know where our next Dream Door Adventure will take us."

"Okay. Here goes." Adam pointed the Dream Doodler, closed his eyes and waved it as he pushed the button.

At once a Dream Door portal opened in the air. It showed a dark sky with horrible lightening and frightening thunder. In the blinding flashes Adam caught a glimpse of what appeared to be a wide, flat, wet wooden roof. And then the scene changed. The portal showed violent waves and then a splash and down, down, down the scene went until finally it showed the muddy bottom of a deep sea. The water was murky with seaweed waving back and forth.

"We have to go there?" Zonia didn't sound so excited now. She sounded terrified.

Molly Beam said worriedly, "Now we know why it came back to us wet and covered in seaweed."

Adam gulped. "Do we have to go to the bottom of the sea, Zekor?"

Zekor laughed and the light that encircled him pulsed gold, green and yellow. "Do you know what you just saw?"

Adam, Zonia, Mom and Dad shook their heads. Staring at the underwater world in the Dream Door portal. The portal slowly closed and winked out.

Zekor said, "You will have an exciting new adventure for sure."

"But where?" Adam asked.

"I don't want to go into that horrible stormy sea," Zonia said.

"You need not to go into the sea, little one. I think you will find the two thieves who stole the apples inside . . ." he paused and smiled at the wondering looks upon their faces. ". . . inside Noah's Ark."

Chapter 4

ADAM FELT A BURST OF EXCITEMENT. "NOAH'S ARK! Quantum."

Toby rose up on his hind legs and stretched, placing two giant paws on the Lighton's shoulders, and stared pleading into the light-being's eyes.

Zekor laughed. "Yes, Toby, you can go too."

"Quantum," Zonia said. "Is it true that the Ark was filled with animals?"

Adam said, "It's all true." He took the large model Ark down from the shelf and showed it to them. "God told Noah to build a huge ship that looked just like this one. Inside it Noah and his family, and two of every kind of air-breathing animals lived in safety until the Great Flood was over."

"That's right," Adam's dad said. "And because God saved only Noah and his family, we all are descended from him and his three sons, Shem, Japheth, and Ham."

"We're like one big family," Molly Beam noted, smiling.

"If we are, why did those two thieves steal the apples from us?" Adam asked.

Zekor crossed his massive arms across his chest leaving sparkling trail of light dancing in the air. "Throughout history, humans have not treated other humans as brothers and sisters. They let the small things turn them into enemies. Maybe the shape of their face, or the color of their skin. It's because of Adam's disobedience. Remember your last Dream Door adventure, how sad he felt when he told you about how he and Eve ate from the only forbidden tree in the whole Garden?"

"I remember," Adam said. "I hoped now, with the Great King ruling the world, that people would treat each other like real brothers and sisters."

Zekor shook his head sadly. "Someday they will. But for now, humans still have to live with their natural selves."

"But not the Brightons?" Zonia asked.

"Not the Brightons. Although they were once as you are. In the Before Time, at the time of the great Taking Away, they were changed. Now they do not sin because they have no desire to sin."

Bud Beam said, "And someday we will be like that too. But for now, we live in these earthy bodies."

"What about you, Zekor?" Adam asked.

Zekor said, "I had to make a choice too, just as you do. I chose to follow the Great King, but many of my kind chose not to." He looked sad. "We all have to make our own choices."

"I choose the Great King," Zonia declared.

"I do too," Adam added.

"And so do we," Bud Beam said, putting an arm around his wife.

Adam said, "I wonder what those two thieves choose?"

Zekor said, "They are still undecided. I hope they make the correct choice soon."

Adam felt sad. He hoped the two thieves would make the right choice too. And then he thought about their next Dream Door Adventure. *Noah's Ark! Quantum!* "Let's get started," he said excitedly.

"Hold up there, young man," His father said. "It's still the middle of the night, and you and Zonia are still in your pajamas."

"We can change quickly," Zonia said. She was anxious to see all the animals on the Ark.

Molly Beam shook her head. "Not so quickly, Zonia. You haven't even had your breakfast."

"Oh mom," Adam and Zonia said together.

Zekor laughed. "Your mom is right. Breakfast is the most important meal of the day. You don't want to skip it. And anyway, there's no need to rush off at once. With the Dream Doodler you can dream draw yourself into any time period at all. You might even arrive on Noah's Ark before those two confused young men."

"He's right. Quantum!" Adam looked at his sister whose arm hugged Toby's thick orange-fur neck. "Maybe we can get there first and catch the thieves when they arrive?"

"You might very well do that." Zekor whole body glowed brighter. "But for this adventure, you will need a special gift from the Great King."

Zonia said, "He knows about the theft already?"

The light enveloping Zekor gleamed and sparkled green and gold beams of light that made Adam's room glow. "The Great King knows everything."

"Then why didn't He stop those bad thieves," Zonia asked.

Bud Beam said, "I think I know the answer to that." He looked at Zekor who nodded that Mr. Beam should continue.

"It's because humans have free will, and they have to decide for themselves if they will be good or bad. If the Great King forced everyone to be good, humans would become like robots. That's not what the Great King wants. He doesn't want robots to follow and love him. He wants real people who love Him all on their own." Bud Beam looked up at Zekor.

The giant Lighton said, "That's exactly right."

"Why don't we all go down stairs for some hot chocolate?" Molly Beam said. "I don't think any of us will be able to go back to sleep tonight, and soon it will be morning."

"Zekor too," Zonia asked.

Mrs. Beam smiled. "Zekor too."

Adam put the model of Noah's Ark back on the shelf, excited about their next Dream Door adventure. Noah and the Great Flood had to be one of his favorite Bible stories, and now he was going to see the real Ark and meet the real Noah!

He could hardly wait.

Almost more than that, he was excited to learn about the special gift the Great King had told Zekor to give to him and his sister.

MOLLY BEAM MADE sure her Adam and Zonia were properly dressed for their next adventure. She prepared a special lunch for them, and packed it in a backpack, along with a rain poncho and two extra pairs of sock in case their feet got wet.

"Mom," Adam sighed when she suggested rubber rain boots. "We won't need those."

Bud Beam smiled at his wife and said, "They will only be away for a few moments. That's the way Dream Doors work."

Zekor wore a small grin, but his eyes were wide with approval for Molly's attentiveness to her children. "You needn't worry, Mrs. Beam. I will keep a close watch over Adam, Zonia, and Toby. As a Dream Door Lighton, that's my job."

"Well, all right . . . I suppose."

"We're ready." Adam buckled the Dream Doodler holster around his waist and Zonia slipped the small backpack over her shoulders. Toby nuzzled between the two of them and sat on the kitchen floor, his great orange tail swishing back and forth.

Zonia laughed. "Toby is ready too."

Zekor said, "One last thing." His rumbling voice was both deep and gentle at the same time. "The Great King's gift." He held out a hand that was a large as a dinner plate. Upon it a wisp of colored light sparked to life and swirled about, growing larger and brighter; red to green to gold. And then the light faded and two little golden objects glinted in the Lighton's palm.

"What are they?" Zonia asked, wonderment in her voice.

"These are your donkey pendants." Zekor handed them to the children.

Adam held his by its golden chain. Thea beautiful golden donkey was about the length of his thumb. He thought it a strange gift from the Great King, and looked questioningly up at Zekor.

"Read what is written upon the donkey."

Adam and Zonia turned their pendants over. On the back sides words glowed with a soft bluish light. Adam recognized them as a Bible verse he'd learned from mom and dad, and from his lessons in Exploretime. "If you ask anything in my name, I will do it."

Zonia said, "That comes from the book of John, chapter 14 and verse 14."

Bud Beam nodded with approval. "Very good, Sunshine. You are exactly right."

"But what does the donkey mean?" Adam asked, looking all over it for a clue.

Zekor laughed. "That, my dear children, is a riddle. You'll need to know your Bible verses to solve it, and solve it you must for your Dream Door adventure to be successful." He winked at the children. "I am confident you two will figure out the puzzle. Now, time to begin."

The morning sky was brightening with a golden light and the brilliant cityscape of Gloriania caught its gleam like a million jewels cast across the green and golden land. Molly Beam felt a little more comfortable now. The middle of the night was no time to begin an adventure, even a Dream Door adventure, which could take them into the middle of the day or into the middle of the night. Even so, she still worried with a motherly worry . . . just a little. "I know you and Adam and Toby will have a fun adventure."

Adam drew the Dream Doodler from its holster. It had a long handle on one end with three large buttons, and a pearly cone on the other end. The green button was labeled "DREAM DRAW". The red button was labeled "OUT." And the blue one was "DISAPPEAR DAZZLER." Adam had used all three of them on their last adventure to the First Time where they rescued the sack of apples from the evil Evols.

He sighed, remembering that adventure. Now he and Zonia and Toby were going to have to rescue those precious apples all over again.

Toby growled excitedly. He was anxious for another Dream Door adventure too!

Adam stood between Zonia and Toby. "Okay, let's start!"

Zekor said, "Imagine the inside of Noah's Ark the way you've seen pictures of it in your Explore-time cube. You don't want to arrive outside the Ark as those two thieves did."

"Okay." Adam closed his eyes and tried to recall exactly the pictures he'd seen. Noah's Ark had been a huge boat, larger than all the houses on his street placed next to each other. He remembered it had three levels, like a towering barn, with staircases and heavy wooden beams, and glowing balls of light that made the big boat almost as bright as daylight. He remembered the cages for the animals; big cages for baboons and lions, small cages for birds and lizards. And there were the stalls where horses and giraffes and elephants and baby dinosaurs stayed.

And there were big rooms filled with hay and straw and oats and barley. Adam gathered together all the details that he could remember and when he was ready, he waved the Dream Doodler in the air and pressed the green **DREAM DRAW** button.

Right there in the middle of Mom's kitchen a dream portal opened up. In it was the very picture that had been in Adam's head.

"Quantum," Zonia said.

"Amazing," Adam's dad said.

Adam said, "Now, quickly, before the portal closes." The two children and Toby leaped through the dream portal. The last thing Adam heard his Mom saying was, "Be careful."

Chapter 5

THEIR FEET THUMPED THE ROUGH WOODEN DECK OF the Ark. The floor pitched back and forth, and sometimes felt like an elevator rising quickly.

"Quantum," Zonia said in awe, grabbing Adam's arm to steady herself. She looked around. "Where are we exactly, Adam?"

"The last picture in my mind was the hay storage bins at the back of the Ark." He was whispering as his view roamed this shadowy corner where the light from the large globes barely reached. High overhead was a dark roof of heavy wooden planks. "That must be the top floor to the deck above." He recalled that the hay had been stored on the second deck.

Toby sniffed and let out a low, cautious growl.

Adam said, "You smell all the animals, don't you Toby?"

The giant Siberian Tiger's orange tail swished back and forth, and walked around the big pile of hay, sniffing.

Zonia wrinkled her nose. "I smell the animals too."

The place did smell a little gamy, but not near as bad as he had imagined it would be. "Come on, let's explore."

There was a commotion behind them and Toby leaped back, startled. A big mouse burst from the hay pile and scurried away.

Adam and Zonia laughed. "Why did it run away from us?" Zonia asked.

"We're no longer in New Eden Time where all the animals are friendly."

"Oh yeah. I forgot. It's the same as our last Dream Door Adventure when the children in Grandfather Adam's time were afraid of Toby." She hugged the tiger's neck. "But you wouldn't hurt even a mouse, would you?"

Toby made a growl that Zonia knew meant *I wouldn't even hurt a mouse*. She also knew that if she or Adam needed to be protected, Toby would be right at their side.

They ventured out of the shadows, moving toward the brighter light, passing barrels and boxes stacked all the way to the ceiling; the supplies for Noah's voyage. They stood in neat rows with wide aisles between them. Each mountain of supplies was covered in a heavy net and anchored to the floor with thick ropes tied to big iron rings.

Adam heard a soft whirring sound. Toby's ears perked. "What's that?" Zonia asked.

Before Adam could answer, a yellow and green tricycle-like machine rushed into view, buzzing like a herd of bees. A man sat upon the machine, steering around one of the mountains of wooden boxes. Attached to the back of the machine was a bright blue cart where another man sat, holding tight.

Just then the men spied Adam, Zonia, and Toby. The tricycle screeched to a halt.

The driver cried, "By Methuselah's beard! Where'd you come from?"

The man in the blue cart hopped out, and then spotted Toby and stopped. He stared at fierce-looking tiger with worry in his eyes.

Adam said quickly, "Toby won't hurt you. He's our friend."

"How did he get out of his cage?" the man sitting on the machine asked.

Adam said, "He was never in a cage."

The two men looked at each other. "Stow-aways," they said, coming to the same conclusion at the same instant.

"We're not stowaways," Zonia said. "We just arrived."

"Impossible."

"Nothing is impossible for the Great King," Adam said.

"Who?" the one standing asked.

"The Creator of all things," Adam said quickly, recalling that was the name by which Grandfather Adam knew the Great King.

The man sitting on the machine let his jaw drop. "By Methuselah's beard," he said again, but this time with awe in his voice instead of surprise. "*He* sent you?"

"We've come on a very important mission," Zonia said.

Toby gave a small growl of agreement and shook his massive orange head.

The men were silent a moment, and then the one standing said, "Pop needs to be told at once."

"Aye, Shem." He hadn't taken his eyes off the children.

"You're Shem?" Zonia asked.

"I am. And who exactly are you?"

"My name is Zonia Beam, and this is my brother, Adam. And this is Toby."

Adam said to the other man, "If he's Shem, you're either Japheth or Ham."

His eyes narrowed suspiciously. "Ham," he agreed cautiously. "How did you know?"

"Oh, you're famous. We learned all about you and your father, Noah, in Exploretime."

"Come with us," Ham said. "You can ride in

the hauler with me." He looked at Toby, a little unsure. "He's too big to fit. You sure he's tame?"

"He wouldn't hurt a fly," Zonia assured him.

"Or a mouse," Adam added and the two of them giggled. "Toby can run fast. He'll follow us."

They climbed into the blue cart and soon they were zipping around lumpy tarps covering strange machines. They zigzagged past mounds of boxes and towers of wooden barrels. Toby easily kept up with them, bounding along a few paces behind the blue cart.

Soon they were zipping down a wide aisle along one side of the huge Ark. Here were rows of stalls for large animals. Adam didn't know the names of all of them, but they were familiar. He'd seen many of them running wild in Gloriania. Some of them, he had learned in Exploretime, had become extinct in the Before Time. Happily, when the Great King returned to rule the world, He brought all the extinct animals back to life and restored their peaceable nature. The world was turning back to as it had been in the First Time, when He'd created it.

Shem steered the machine onto a wide ramp. Adam and Zonia held tight as the cart careened to one side. They rushed up to a landing, made a sharp turn and then up another ramp to the third floor.

Here the cages were smaller and packed closer together. They held animals of all shapes, sizes, and colors: Birds and monkeys, aardvarks and hedgehogs, goats and sheep, and lots of different snakes and small furry creatures. The cart zoomed by so quickly, Adam didn't have time to identify them all.

The Ark was so big that zipping around the rows of cages was like trying to find the way through a hedge maze. Adam was all turned around. Overhead, dark, stormy light came through the long, low rows of windows. A cold wind whistled through them, filling the air with a wet mist.

The electric whine of the yellow-green machine changed pitch and they came to a stop in front of a tall and wide doorway. Adam heard voices coming from beyond the door, and warm, cheery light spilled out onto the rough deck at their feet.

"Come along," Shem said, looking warily at Toby.

"Can Toby come too?" Zonia asked.

"He's really very friendly," Adam added.

Shem looked at Ham. "What do you think?"

"I suppose he can come along — if he's as friendly as you say."

They stepped through the doorway and immediately the air was warmer. It was a big room with a large table in the middle and counters and cabinets along one wall. A fire burned in an odd clay fireplace against another wall. On the third wall was a stove and a sink where two women were preparing food. A man sat at the table flipping through a thick stack of papers. A long hallway ran along one side and as Adam looked down it, another man strode slowly down it, peering at an odd, shiny machine in his hands. The machine sparkled like green crystal and golden glints. It reminded Adam a little of the light that shown continually from the Great Kings throne room.

He was an older man, with dark, curly hair and a short beard that showed a little gray. He looked up just then and saw Adam and Zonia. He stopped sharply and cried, "Impossible!" He peered at them more intently. "Be you flesh and blood, or messengers from the Creator of All?"

This was Noah himself! Adam recognized him from the live images of him he'd seen in the Exploretime History Vision Cube.

"Found these three hiding amongst the hay stacks, Pop," Shem said.

Noah was staring at Toby. Toby gave a low, friendly growl and rolled onto his back. Zonia scratched his tummy to demonstrate how tame Toby really was. The room filled with his rumbling purr.

By now everyone there had gathered round Adam and Zonia. Noah set the sparkling machine on the table and then stood over the children. "How did you get aboard my boat?"

Adam showed him the Dream Doodler. "We used this, sir. It's called a Dream Doodler. We have come from the future."

"By Methuselah's beard!" Noah suddenly

looked worried. "Are you of the Serpent Clan or a follower of the Creator of All?"

"Zonia said, "Oh, we definitely follow the Creator, Mr. Noah. Where we come from, He's called the Great King."

"Why have you come to us? Are you on an important task for the Great Cre-, I mean the Great King?"

"We are," Adam said. "You see, we had just got back from rescuing Adam's Apples, when two bad people stole them. They Dream Doodled themselves here, onto Noah's Ark."

Noah's eyes went wide and there was excitement in his voice. "Ah, so you are the two from the future! I recall the story now. Grandfather Methuselah told it to me. He'd been told the story by his father, Grandfather Enoch."

Zonia said, "Enoch was just a little boy when he helped us rescue the apples from the evil Evols." She frowned sadly. "And now we have to rescue them again."

Noah said, "There is no one but the eight of us aboard my ship." He looked around at the others, who all shook their head. At that moment a third and fourth woman entered the room, and stopped, shocked to see the children and the Big tiger rolling on the floor, scratching its back.

"Naamah, Kitah," Noah said, "These children have been sent to us from the Creator of All. They are on an important mission to find the apples that Grandfather Adam brought out of the Garden!"

There was excited talk all around. Noah introduced the man who'd been sitting at the table. He was Noah's third son, Japheth. The two women who'd been cooking were Desmorah and Majiah.

Majiah was Ham's wife. Kitah was Shem's wife. And Desmorah was married to Japheth. Naamah was Mrs. Noah.

Toby nuzzled in amongst them and soon the wives were petting him and the husbands admiring the powerful animal that was as gentle as their pet pussy cat named Stalker. Stalker had emerged from a dark corner to see what all the excitement was all about.

Adam had lots of questions about the Ark, and Noah promised to give them a tour of the big boat after dinner. Adam wasn't very hungry because he'd just eaten breakfast not half an hour earlier, but he happily joined the family around the table as dinner was served.

The food was cooked the old fashion way on a hot stove and served in big bowls, like Mom sometimes cooked for very special occasions. Usually, their food simply appeared in the Manna Manger on the kitchen counter. That was how it was done in New Eden Time.

Toby was given a big bowl of the same food Stalker ate, and tiger and pussy cat ate together.

Stalker somehow understood that Toby was a gentle friend, and not a ferocious foe.

The family held hands and Noah prayed a prayer of thanksgiving to the Creator of All. He thanked Him for the good food, the protection that they had inside the Ark, and especially for their three unexpected quests from the far future.

Chapter 6

"BUT THERE *ARE* NO OTHER PEOPLE ABOARD THE Ark," Japheth said for the third time as everyone ate. He looked at Adam. "Are you certain the two thieves arrived here?"

"Yes, sir," Adam said. "The Dream Doodler records everything that happens. And Zekor said this is where the two ended up. But I think we got here before they did."

"Ah, very clever" Noah said. "Now that we know they are coming, we can be prepared."

"Yes sir, Mr. Noah. I think that's why Zekor arranged for us to arrive ahead of them."

"Who is Zekor?" Desmorah asked.

Adam said, "He our Exploretime Lighton. I believe you'd call him a messenger. Lightons were known by many names in the First Time."

Noah said, "Well, we'll be prepared when these two scoundrels arrive."

After dinner Noah and Ham gave Adam and Zonia a tour of the Ark. Toby stayed in the kitchen with the women because they kept throwing him scraps of food from the plates as they scraped and washed them.

"This is amazing," Adam said looking all around at the cages and stalls. "How many animals do you have inside here?"

Noah chuckled at the children's wide, wondering eyes. "I don't know for sure. You see, the Creator of All sent them to us, we didn't have to go catch them ourselves. Of course, we tried to count them as they came, but toward the end they came so quickly, and we had so much to do, that we didn't get a complete count. Counting them is what Japheth is doing now."

"How do you feed them all?" Zonia asked.

Noah made a weary sigh. "Feeding them and cleaning up after them is a full day's work every day. We only ever rest on the Seventh Day, and even then something always comes up for us to do. But we do have help."

Noah pointed to gleaming pipes running over the stalls that they were walking past. "Ham designed the water works that keeps the bowls filled with fresh water. That saves us from a lot of work. And that down there," he pointed at a big turning drum that look like a huge screw, "takes all the waste away and moves it down below where it goes into big tanks that turn it into gas. The gas runs our machines, gives us our heat, and cooks our food."

"Quantum," Adam said, his eyes darting this way and that. He had always thought of the Ark as simply a big boat with lots of animals crowded everywhere. He never thought it might be filled with all kinds of clever machines as well.

Ham said, "It was all quite simple, really. The difficult part was building the wind machine that moves fresh air through the ark. See?" He pointed. "That's it over there."

"Wind machine?" Adam didn't see a machine. What he saw was a big square box that went from the floor to the very top of the Ark.

"We call it the *Deep Pool*," Noah said.

A stout, wooden staircase climbed around the outside of the four walls of the big box. Halfway up the stairs Noah stopped at a window where the children could peer inside the box.

Adam and Zonia pressed their noses to the glass. Beyond it water sloshed back and forth with the movement of the Ark. The water rose up and up until it almost reached the top. And then it dropped down, down, down. When it did, Adam saw that the box went all the way through the floor to the bottom of the boat.

With the next big wave, the water rushed up again, and when it did Adam felt a strong wind blow through the Ark. And as the water fell down,

down, down again, another strong wind blew through the Ark in a different direction.

Adam said, "It's an air big pump."

"That's exactly what it is," Ham declared. "It uses the up and down motion of the Ark to move air throughout the boat."

"That is very clever," Zonia said.

Noah puffed out his chest and grinned. "My boy Ham is a very clever fellow."

Noah took the children around the boat showing them many of the animals that the Creator of All had sent to be saved from the flood. There were tiny mice and scruffy moles with funny noses, rabbits and badgers, beavers and foxes, sheep and kangaroos, horses and giraffes, and elephants, rhinoceroses and even baby dinosaurs.

When they got back to the big kitchen, Toby was playing with Stalker. Japheth was at the table again, writing on the papers in front of him. Kitah was the only other person there, strumming an odd harp-like instrument that made beautiful music.

Mrs. Noah came down the long hallway carrying blankets and pillows. "You children can sleep here in the Gathering Room tonight," she said. "I sent Shem to fetch some hay to make a soft mattress."

She'd just finished speaking when a big wave hit the ark and tipped it steeply to one side. A distant crash followed by a faint cry reached their ears. It could only have come from Shem.

"Shem!" Naamah said and looked at Noah with sudden concern on her face. Everyone rushed out the doorway in the directions of Shem's cry.

Zonia's shorter legs couldn't keep up. Toby came alongside her and crouched low so that she could leap onto his back. Soon Toby and Zonia were running alongside the others, racing quickly down the ramp and along one of the Ark's dimly lit corridors past mounds of supplies. Adam recognized it as the same place Zonia, Toby, and he had arrived inside the Ark only a few hours earlier.

Back where the hay and straw had been stacked in tall plies, dark, heavy beams of wood blocked their way. Beneath it, crushed flat, was the little yellow green machine. Boxes and barrels and can lay scattered across the floor. Iron tools and gooey green liquid were spilled all over the place.

But there was no sight of Shem anywhere.

"One of the storage shelves fell away from the wall," Ham said. "That big wave broke off the mounting brackets."

Noah called, "Shem! Shem, can you hear me?"

Shem didn't answer, but Adam heard a faint groan coming from someplace beneath the huge, heavy shelving. "He must be trapped under these timbers."

Kitah said, "I hear him. He might be hurt." Her words were choked with fear.

"Let's lift this shelving," Noah said, and he and

Ham and Japheth tried to lift the huge timbers, but they didn't budge.

"What can we do to help them, Adam?" Zonia asked.

Adam looked all around, and then he spied something up in the shadowy ceiling rafters high overhead. It looked like a big pulley hanging from a strong chain.

"Mr. Noah, what is that up there?"

Noah looked up from his groaning and grunting from trying to move the heavy shelf. "Ah! Of course! A block and tackle. Quick, Ham, fetch a rope."

Ham found a thick rope wrapped in coils. He put it over his shoulder and climbed a ladder to a narrow catwalk overhead. In short order, he threaded the rope through the big pulley. Noah and Japheth tied it onto the fallen shelf.

Ham slid down the other end of the rope and when his feet hit the floor everyone grabbed hold of the rope and pulled on it together.

The massive shelf moved a little, but that was all. "It's too heavy," Zonia cried.

Adam remembered all the stalls they'd passed on their way here. "We can use one of the animals to pull," he suggested.

Ham said, "None of them has been taught to pull a load. They might become frightened. I'm afraid they'd make even more trouble for us."

Beneath the heavy shelved, Seth groaned again.

"We have to try," Majiah and Kitah said at the same time.

"If only there was some way to explain it to the animal," Desmorah said, but she sounded hopeless.

Shem's voice came weakly. "Hello. Can anyone hear me?"

Noah said, "We hear you son. We're working to free you now. Are you badly hurt?"

"My head hurts. I think I was knocked out. Wa-what happened?"

"One of the storage shelves broke loose," Noah said.

Ham shook his head. "I don't understand how it could have happened. I designed the mounting fixtures myself. They are made of the finest steel I could buy."

Shem groaned again. His wife Kitah said, "The animals are our only hope. We must give it a try."

Adam said, "I saw a pair of elephants back there in a stall."

"How will an elephant know what we want it to do?" Noah asked worriedly. "Ham is right. If it becomes frightened it might do more harm than good."

Just then both Adam and Zonia heard Zekor's voice speaking inside their heads. *Children, remember the special gift the Great King gave you?*

Zonia and Adam looked at each other. "Did you hear that?" Adam whispered to his sister.

Zonia nodded and then looked at Noah and his

family. She whispered back, "But no one else heard Zekor."

Noah and the others tried again to lift the heavy shelving, pulling hard on the rope, the heavy shelf refused to budge.

"Zekor mentioned the special gift from the Great King," Adam whispered and took the shiny, metal donkey from his pocket. "What do you suppose he meant?"

Zonia said, "Remember, he said it was a puzzle."

Adam turned the donkey pendant over and read the words on the backside again. "If you ask anything in my name, I will do it."

"What do these words have to do with a donkey?" Zonia asked.

Adam shrugged. "Zekor said it was a puzzle so let's figure it out. The donkey has to be a clue."

Zonia said, "We were taught that once, long ago, the Great King rode into Jerusalem on a Donkey."

"That's in the Bible," Adam said. "And since the Bible is the Great King's word, that must be where we will find the answer to our puzzle."

Zonia and Adam's foreheads scrunched as they thought. Zonia said, "Samson fought the Philistines with the jaw of a donkey."

Adam thought about that, but he didn't see how that might apply to the problem of helping Noah rescue Shem. He tried to remember all the Bible stories he'd been taught about the Before Time. "Abigail rode a donkey when she visited David."

Zonia shook her head. "Back then everyone rode donkeys. That doesn't help much."

"You're right." Adam thought some more. "What about not plowing a field with a donkey and ox yoked together? It says that somewhere in the Bible."

Zonia said, "Noah has a donkey and an ox here. Maybe we are supposed to use them to help Noah?"

"But the Bible says we are not supposed to use a donkey and ox together," Adam reminded her.

"Oh, yeah. That's right. Hum?" She looked at the donkey pendant again. "What other famous person used a donkey?"

The answer sprang into Adam's head. "Balaam! Remember when he disobeyed God, God made the donkey able to speak, to warn him of the Lighton standing in the road with his sword?"

"That must be it, Adam," Zonia said excitedly. She looked back at the donkey pendant. "This pendant is to remind us that the Great King can open the mouths of animals so that we can talk to them!"

Chapter 7

ADAM AND ZONIA RAN THE ROWS OF STALLS WHERE all different kinds of animals lived. They stopped in front of a stout enclosure where two young elephants were scooping up hay with their trunks and eating.

Zonia pointed the donkey pendant at the elephants and said, "Talk to us."

But the elephants just kept eating the hay in their feed troughs.

Zonia looked at the pendant. "It's not working."

"There's a message on the back side, remember?" Adam turned it over and read the message again. He said, "The pendant says all we have to do is ask."

"Let's try," Zonia said.

The children said aloud, "Great King, please open the mouth of this elephant like you did to Balaam's donkey."

"Whoa! Suddenly my head is swimming," one of the elephants said, his voice deep and rumbly. He staggered a bit as swung his trunk, looking around, startled.

"You can talk!" Adam declared.

The elephant gasped and stumbled backed into the side of the stall, rattling the timbers. He stated at the children and his eyes got big. "You can talk?" He squeaked.

Zonia laughed. "Of course we can talk. We always talk. But elephants don't talk."

He nudged the second elephant there, "Tibbi, do you hear what I hear?"

Tibbi continued eating contentedly. If she was aware of what had happened to her mate, she gave no sign of it.

"I don't think she can talk," Adam said. He was mildly shocked too, but not surprised. The Great King could do anything — even make an elephant talk, maybe even fly, if He had wanted to.

"Well, why can I talk and my Tibbi not?" His deep, rumbly voice had returned, and as he spoke his trunk gently prodded his neck as if becoming aware of the new sensation of speech coming from that part of his anatomy.

"Because we need your help, and the Great King has given you the ability to understand us."

The elephant's eyes narrowed in sudden deep thought. "I know the Great King, but don't ask me how I know."

"It's instinct," Adam said. "Everyone knows about the Great King, only, some don't want to admit it. At least that's what my Exploretime teacher, Mrs. Levin, told us. But she was telling us about the Before Time. In New Eden Time everyone knows the Great King."

"Woo-hoo. I want to go to New Eden Time." The elephant raised his trunk and trumpeted. Tibbi looked up at him briefly, and then went back to eating her dinner.

"Well, maybe someday you will. But right now we need your help. Will you help us?"

"Of course, little ones. Err, but what do you want me to help you do?"

Zonia said, "A heavy shelf fell on Mr. Shem and we can't lift it."

"Shem!" Sudden concern flashed in the elephant's dark brown eyes. "Of course I'll help you."

Adam lifted the heavy latch and swung the gate wide open.

"Be back in two shakes, Tibbi!" he said and thumped put the gate.

Tibbi turned to follow, but Adam quickly shut and latched the gate. She didn't seem to mind and slowly turned back to the pile of hay she was eating by the trunk-full.

The children started quickly back to where Noah and his family were trying to rescue Shem. "My name is Adam, and this is my sister, Zonia."

"I'm Bugarah," the big animal said, his heavy footsteps thumping on the wooden floor. "I haven't seen you two before."

"That's because we only just arrived," Zonia said.

Noah and the others were still struggling to lift the shelf when they arrived.

"We've brought reinforcements," Adam shouted.

Noah turned with startled surprise in his eyes. Japheth and Ham stepped forward as though to protect Noah from the charging animal chasing Adam and Zonia.

"It's okay," Adam said. He's going to help us.

Ham said, "But I already told you that an untrained animal will cause more problems than-"

"What do you mean, untrained?" Bugarah replied.

Japheth leaped back and nearly fell over the shelf. Ham's jaw dropped to his chest, and Noah grabbed Ham's arm for support. The women all just stared.

Mrs. Noah was the first to regain her tongue. "A talking elephant?"

Bagarah said, "I'll admit it is rather unusual now that I think about it, but nothing is too difficult for the Great King and Creator."

Mrs. Noah looked to be in shock and had nothing to say to that.

Bagarah chuckled a deep rumble. "Tell me what to do, Noah?"

Noah stammered and said finally, "You know my name?"

"Of course! You and Ham there and Japheth, and all the others visit me and Tibbi every day. You give us fresh food, make sure the stream is flowing clean water to drink, and sweep the floors. I must say, we are very grateful for the fine care you give us. Only, how much longer is this boat ride going to last? Sometimes I get funny in the stomach from all the bobbing back and forth."

Noah and his son looked at each other in amazement.

Adam said, "Bagarah, we need you to grab that rope and pull back on it." He pointed at the rope and the pulley way us in the ceiling rafters.

Bagarah understood immediately. "Move aside. Give me some room." He took the rope in his powerful trunk, gave it a couple turns and then took a step backward. The rope went taunt and with a groan of wood, the heavy shelf lifted a few inches. Another backward step and the shelf was high enough for Japheth and Ham to duck under it and rush to Shem's side.

"Hurry now," Bagarah said. "This is a heavy load even for me."

Shem was crouched alongside the tractor-like machine, which had been crushed nearly flat. Luckily, the machine had stopped the shelf before it had seriously hurt Shem.

Japheth and Ham helped him crawl out from under the heavy timbers. Shem's wife, Kitah, gave him a big hug. "Are you all right?"

Shem pressed a hand to his forehead where big cut was bleeding. "I was knocked unconscious for a while, but the mechmule saved my life."

Adam said to Bagarah, "You can let go now."

Bagarah moved forward and the shelf settled back on the mechmule with the sound of crunching metal.

Noah said, "Thank you, thank you. You were a great help, Bagarah."

Everyone gathered around the elephant and petted him, and reached and scratched him behind the ears. Toby purred and rubbed against Bagarah's leg.

"Woo-hoo, I'm just like family!"

"Yes you are," Kitah said.

Bagarah gently wrapped his trunk around her and gave her a big elephant hug.

Zonia said, "You were wonderful."

Bagarah lifted his trunk and trumpeted. From far back in the ark, Tibbi trumpeted back. Bagarah said, "Tibbi is wondering where I got off too."

Noah said to Adam and Zonia, "You two take Bagarah back to his stall now."

"Come on, Bagarah," Zonia said.

The elephant thumped along behind the children. Toby trotted ahead of them. "I'm feeling a little light headed again. Woo-hoo. Hey, this is a pretty big boat."

"It has to be," Zonia said. "There has to be room to save every kind of animal from the Flood."

"Every kind of air-breathing animal," Adam explained. "You see, God, the Creator and Great King, had to cleanse the world of a horrible sin."

"And what better way to clean than with water?" Zonia added.

They reached Bagarah's stall and Adam opened the stout gate. "Can we come back and visit with you later?" he asked.

Bagarah didn't reply. Adam turned. The big elephant stood there staring at Adam in an empty-eyed way.

"Bagarah? What's wrong?" Adam asked worriedly. "Hello. Bagarah?"

But Bagarah didn't appear to have heard him as he lumbered heavily back into his pen.

Zonia said, "I don't think he can understand us anymore, Adam."

Toby gave a sad growl and peered between the thick rails at the elephant.

Adam sighed and shut the gate. "I guess animals aren't meant to talk to people. The Great King permitted Bagarah to talk because He knew we needed help." He took the donkey pendant from his pocket and looked at it. "Well, at least we solved the riddle."

"Zekor knew we would," Zonia said.

The children watched Bagarah a moment longer hoping the friendly elephant would say goodbye or something. He didn't. He'd gone back to the pile of hay and seemed happy just to be next to Tibbi again.

Adam said, "Let's see how Mr. Seth is feeling."

Chapter 8

"THIS HAS BEEN A MOST UNUSUAL DAY," NOAH SAID while Kitah and Naamah wrapped a clean white bandage around Seth's forehead. "First we have the arrival of Adam, Zonia, and Toby the friendly tiger; visitors from the future. And then Seth's accident with the shelf. And finally a talking elephant! I wonder what else can happen?"

Ham said, "I don't understand how the shelf could have broken loose, pop. I built and installed the brackets that hold it in place myself. It shouldn't have happened."

Adam had been thinking about the accident and he had a funny feeling about it. He'd seen the steel brackets Ham had built and they looked strong enough to hold . . . to hold an elephant." He smiled to himself thinking again of Bagarah. But it made him suspicious. Had it really been an accident?"

"I wonder," Adam said aloud.

Everyone in the big gathering room looked at him. "What do you wonder?" Noah asked.

"Well, could someone have caused the accident? Someone who wanted to hurt Seth?"

Noah looked startled. "Impossible. There are only the eight of us here — and you two. Who could possibly want to hurt Seth?"

Adam said, "How about the Evols?"

Zonia hugged Toby's beck and said, "Oh no. Can they really be here?"

Adam said, "Evols are like Lightons. They can appear and disappear almost anywhere they want to. Remember how they appeared in the secret room in the cave where the Apples were hidden?"

Japheth's eyes narrowed worriedly. "The Evols are the beings who brought so much evil into our world that the Creator of All had to destroy it. We are the only ones left. It would make sense that the Evols would want to get rid of us too."

"Whatever shall we do?" Majiah asked. "If it's true, then we are all in danger."

Noah said reasonably, "If the Creator of All chose to spare us from the evil that the Evols brought upon the old world, it makes sense He will protect us now and see us safely to the other side of our voyage, to the new world that awaits us."

Shem said, "That's true, pop. But that doesn't mean they can't cause mischief during the voyage."

"What would be the point?" Desmorah asked.

Adam said, "I have an idea. The Evols want the

special apples Grandfather Adam took from the Garden of Eden. Maybe they know that the thieves who stole the apples from my bedroom are coming here?"

Noah said, "If that's true, the arrival of the thieves must be soon."

"My guess too," Adam said. "Zekor would have made sure we arrived close to the time the thieves would arrive."

Ham said, "I'm going back to that shelf and examine those brackets again. If Evols are involved, the bracket will show signs of being tampered with."

"I'll go with you," Japheth said. "I want to start cleaning up that mess."

"You two be careful," Naamah said. "And bring some straw when you come back so that we can make a soft bed for Adam and Zonia."

"And Toby," Zonia added.

Ham and Japheth left, and Noah sat at the big table shaking his head. "Indeed, this has been an unusual day. Why would the Evols be interested in the apples from the Garden?"

Adam said, "The Great King wants to plant them throughout all of Glorainia and New Eden so that all the people might benefit from them."

"But wasn't that Grandfather Adam's great sin? Eating of the fruit of the forbidden tree."

"These apples weren't from *that* tree," Zonia said.

Adam said, "That's right. The apples the thieves stole are from the Tree of Life. The evil one, the one the Evols call *His Magnificence*, wanted to destroy them from the very beginning. That's why the Great King ordered two Cherubim to guard the way to the Tree of Life."

THUMP! THUMP! OOOOPH!

Noah sprang to his feet. The thumps had come from beyond the doorway. "What was that?"

Zonia pointed out the doorway at the row of windows high overhead. "It came from up there."

The planting beds," Shem said.

"The thieves?" Adam suggested.

"Shem and I will check it out. The rest of you stay here."

Noah grabbed an odd-looking flashlight that rested flat on the palm of his hand. The two of them hurried out the door and up steps that led to the growing boxes beneath the long row of window. It was dark up there, except for the lightening that flashed and illuminated the young plants growing in the rich, black soil.

Noah pointed his flashlight far down the dark walkway.

"I'm sure we heard it, father," Shem said loudly.

"Yes, Shem, I heard it too." Then Noah spied something and grinned. He whispered, "I see a couple pair of feet back there behind the planting beds."

Shem grinned and leaned close to his father's ear. "I see them too."

Noah said louder, "But there can be nobody here. We eight are the only people on board."

Shem scratched his head and answered loudly too. "Maybe it's those monkeys again. You know how clever they are. The female has figured out how to undo the latch to their cage."

"Maybe." Something caught Noah's eye. He bent over the planting bed. "Look at this." He held a broken tomato plant in the glow of his palm light. "Ripped right out of the garden. I think you're right, Shem. Let's see if we can find those mischievous monkeys."

They went back down the stairs. Soon as they reached the common room Noah said, "Our two thieves have arrive." He opened a closet door and grabbed a couple of very large butterfly nets, handing one of the nets to Shem. With a chuckle, he added, "We will be right back, and if I'm not mistaken, we won't be empty handed."

Sure enough, a few minutes later Adam heard their approaching footsteps. In came Noah and Shem, and the two thieves with nets down over their heads. One was tall and skinny. The other was short and round. Adam recognized them immediately. These were the same two who had been in his bedroom, the same ones who had stolen Adam's Apples!

The tall, skinny man stared out the net at Adam. "Y-you?"

The other man glared at his partner. "Shut up bonehead. Don't say nothin'."

Toby growled and prowled around the two men sniffing.

Zonia said, "Why did you steal the apples? Don't you know stealing is wrong?"

The taller fellow stammered. "It weren't my idea."

"I said shut up. You're going to get us into more trouble," the shorter man said.

Noah said, "Both of you settle down." They lifted the nets off the two and Noah pointed at chairs. "Sit."

They did. The taller fellow sat near where a cake that had been freshly taken from the oven and was cooling. "I'm really hungry," he said.

"I said shut up," his partner growled again and glared back at Noah, who was studying them closely.

Noah said, "First things first. What are your names?"

"We're not saying."

But the other said, "M-my name is Castor, and this is Lester. An-and were awful sorry to have dropped in on you like this. I-it was a mistake."

Adam said, "Stealing those apples was the mistake. Now you've gotten caught."

Castor looked down, embarrassed. His view traveled back to the cake on the counter.

"Why did you do it?" Zonia asked.

Lester crossed his arms defiantly. "I'm not saying."

Noah glanced at Castor. "How about you? Are you going to talk?"

"Don't say nothin'" Lester warned.

Adam could see that Castor wanted to say more, but that he was afraid of his partner. Adam signaled to Noah and whispered in Noah's ear.

Noah smiled thinly. "It just might work." He bent toward Naamah and said something quietly to her. She nodded and took down a plate from a cabinet and sliced a big piece of the cake.

Noah set the cake on the table just out of Castor's reach. "Now, what do you say we start over, young man?"

Castor licked his lips, staring at the delicious piece of cake. "I'm awful hungry."

Lester opened his mouth to rebuke his friend again, but closed it without saying a word. Instead, he leaned a little closer toward the cake.

Noah struggled to hold back a grin. He said, "Naamah, perhaps another slice of cake is in order?"

She quickly brought over a second plate.

"Now," Noah said, setting the second plate next to the first, "Why did you two steal those apples from Adam and Zonia."

"I don't remember," Lester said.

Castor said, "It w-was Lester's idea."

Adam said, "You were going to give them back to the Evols, weren't you?"

Lester said, "Okay, so we were. What's the big deal over a sack of old apples anyway?" He shut his mouth and refused to say more.

Noah nudged the plates toward Lester and Castor, yet still out of their reach. "Why were you going to give the apples to the Evols."

"I don't know why." Castor said. "T-they just wanted them for some reason. They took them from the First Adam."

Noah looked at Lester. Lester shrugged. "Don't know and don't care. I figured if they wanted 'em bad enough to take 'em in the first place, then maybe they'd pay a reward for getting 'em back."

Noah pulled thoughtfully at his beard. "Hum. So, you took the apples hoping to get reward money from them?"

Castor said, "L-Lester said they'd give us gold." He scratched his head. "Don't know why that matters much since there's so much gold in Gloriania already. I figured Lester knew what he was doing, I guess."

Zonia piped up, "If thieves really knew what they were doing, they wouldn't be thieves."

Lester scowled at her. Toby gave a low, dangerous growl that quickly wiped the scowl from his face.

Noah pushed the two pie plates a little closer. "Okay, so we know you two stole the apples from Adam, and that you hoped to get a reward from the Evols. So, how did you end up here, on my ship?"

Lester pointed a finger at Castor. "It's all his fault. The bonehead had the Dream Doodler and this is where it took us. I told him nobody who flunks Dream Drawing in Exploretime School ought to play with a Dream Doodler."

"I . . . DIDN'T . . . FLUNK!"

"Well, what's done is done. All you have to do is give the apples back to Adam and Zonia, and you can return to where it is you came from. I'm sure the Creator of All -- the Great King as you know Him in your time -- will know how to properly deal with you two."

Lester looked at Castor, and neither young man said anything.

"Well, what are you waiting for," Noah prodded. "Tell us where the apples are and you can each have a piece of cake." He pushed the plates within the reach of the two.

Why they didn't speak? Adam was anxious to get the sack of apples back and then dream draw Zonia, Toby, and these two thieves back to New Eden Time. Whatever punishment the Great King would give Lester and Castor, Adam knew it would be fair.

Castor swallowed and turned his head away from the cake. He lowered his view and peered down at his shoes. "We don't have the apples anymore."

Shem said, "That's pretty obvious. You must have hidden them. Tell me where they are and I'll get them right now."

Lester said, "I would, but you can't get them."

"What do you mean?" Zonia and Adam said at the same time.

"We lost them."

"Oh no!" Zonia cried. "The apples didn't . . . they didn't-"

"They did," Lester said. He turned his thumb down. "*KERPLUNK!* Straight to the bottom, and since this here flood is worldwide, those apples can be anywhere!"

Chapter 9

ADAM WONDERED IF THINGS COULD GET ANY WORSE, and then they did.

Japheth and Ham came back just then. They were surprised to discover Lester and Castor there, but the news they brought was an even greater shock to everyone there.

Ham said, "The steel bracket holding the storage shelf to the side of the ship had been cut."

"Cut!" Noah cried. "No one here would ever do such a thing."

Adam said, "Then it must be true that the Evols are to blame."

Japheth nodded. "Adam might be right. What other explanation can there be?"

Majiah said, "I'm frightened to think that those horrible creatures might be here with us, on the boat."

Ham put an arm around his wife's shoulder.

"We shouldn't be frightened. The Creator of All will protect us."

Desmorah said, "He protected Shem from getting hurt badly when that shelf fell."

Shem touched the bandage around his head. "Desmorah is right. It could have been much, much worse."

Lester looked up from the slice of cake he was shoveling into his mouth and glanced at Castor, a scheme forming in his nasty brain. He inched closer to his buddy and whispered, "Maybe we can make a deal with the Evols right here?"

Castor opened his mouth to protest, but Lester scowled at him and whispered sharply, "Don't say nothing."

Castor closed his mouth. He looked confused, but soon he was back at work eating the cake Noah had finally allowed them to have.

Naamah watched the two young men, and then sighed. "I think we can all do with a slice of cake right now."

Soon Noah's family, along with Lester, Castor, Adam, and Zonia were gathered around the big table, eating cake and discussing what to do next.

Shem said, "We can do a careful search for the lost apples once this flood ends and the land is dry again."

Japheth said, "If it ever does end. It's been raining for a month now."

Majiah said, "It must end sometime. This can't

go on forever."

"I'm sure it will stop," Noah said, "but by then it will be too late. Those apples will be ruined. And even if they do manage to keep, how will we ever find them? Surely they will be buried in deep mud."

Adam said, "Oh, it will end. In Exploretime we learned that the Great Flood lasted one year. And then everyone aboard the Ark stepped out onto dry land."

"One year! Oh my! Well, that's good to know," Kitah said.

Zonia's face looked sad and she didn't have much of an appetite, even though Mrs. Noah's cake was delicious. "But the Flood covered the whole world. Finding a single sack of apples would be even harder than finding a needle in a haystack."

Adam said, "We can't wait that long. We have to do something now."

Lester said, "What can you do now? You would need a big navy to search for the apples."

"That's it!" Adam sprang to his feet, a plan suddenly forming in his brain. Or maybe it was Zekor's voice softly prodding him on?

Toby lifted his big head off his paws and watched Adam pace as he began to put together a plan.

"We need to organize a navy!"

Lester laughed. "Bonehead. How do we do that? There are only-" he quickly counted heads, "- only twelve of us."

"And Toby," Zonia reminded him sternly.

"We can enlist all the animals in all the oceans," Adam countered.

"You're crazy," Lester said.

"Yeah, crazy," Castor parroted and laughed. "A crazy bonehead." He seemed pleased to hear the nasty name used on someone else for a change, instead of himself.

"All we have to do is find a way to talk to one of them. Just like we talked to Bagarah, with this." Adam took the donkey pendent from his pocket and showed it to Lester.

"If I can only talk to a dolphin, he could tell his friends, and before you know it, we'll have a navy of dolphins and whales and fish looking for the apples!"

"That's a wonderful idea," Noah said. "And I think I know just where we might be able to find a dolphin. Come with me. You too, Shem. You other boys stay here and keep an eye on these two thieves."

Noah led the way. Toby bounded along with them, trotting ahead to investigate the wonderful smells coming from row upon row and aisle upon aisle of cages, most holding a single pair of animals. Some larger cages held more than one pair. The dove cage seemed to have a whole flock of doves, cooing loudly as Adam and Zonia hurried past right on Noah's heals.

Adam remembered from his Exploretime

lessons that God had commanded Noah to take two of each kind of animal onto the Ark, but of some special animals called *clean animals*, he was supposed to bring seven pair.

"Doves must be clean animals," he said to Zonia.

She only nodded because she was breathing hard trying to keep up with Noah's long, fast strides.

Soon they came to that huge square room like an elevator shaft in the middle of the Ark that Noah had shown them earlier. Adam remembered it was full of water. Noah called it the deep pool because the bottom was open so that the water could rise and fall within its walls. Shem built it to be a big pump, sweeping fresh air into the Ark and pushing stale air out.

They climbed up the stairs and went through a door at the top of the deep pool shaft onto a small platform high above the water. Adam and Zonia grabbed the safety rail and peered down rising and falling water. Outside the Ark powerful waves roared, but here inside the deep pool shaft the water's surface was only a little choppy. But the wind was terrific!

When the water fell, a tornado of wind swept in from the vents above their heads. And when the water rose, another *whoosh* of wind tornado swept up and out through those same vents.

When it did, Zonia's hair stood straight up. It tickled and she giggled even though the deep pool shaft was kind of scary. Her grip on the safety rail got tighter.

Noah said, "This is the only place in the whole Ark where we can get close to the water."

Adam looked up at him, "I don't see any fish."

Noah nodded. "You're right. I don't see one either." They had to speak loudly to be heard above the roar of wind inside the shaft.

Zonia said, "Maybe Zekor can send one?"

Noah looked surprised. "Who's Zekor? Don't tell me there is someone else aboard my ship?"

Zonia said, "Zekor is our Dream Door Lighton. He keeps an eye on Dream Door adventures, but I don't think he is here. You see, he's one of the Great King's messengers and he can go anywhere the Great King sends him."

Shem said, "How do you talk to Zekor?"

"I just talk to him like I talk to you. He usually answers inside my head, but sometimes everyone can hear him." She thought a moment and then said, "Zekor, can you help us? We need a sea creature to come here so that we can ask it to help us find the Great King's apples that are lost."

Zekor's voice boomed in the deep pool shaft, and this time everyone heard it. "I have already found just the creature for you, Zonia. She's on her way now."

Noah and Shem looked around. "Where is he?" Shem asked.

Adam grinned. "Zekor hardly ever appears in person, not in a Dream Door adventure."

They peered down at the water, waiting for the sea creature Zekor had sent.

"What's taking her so long?" Shem asked after a couple minutes had passed.

"Maybe she had to swim a long way," Adam said.

"There!" Noah pointed to the bluish shadow circling at the bottom of the deep pool. The shadow darted this way and that, and grew larger as it neared the surface. The head of a dolphin lifted above the water and chattered in her dolphin language, which Adam could not understand.

He grabbed the donkey pendant in his pocket and said aloud, "Great King, I pray that you will let this dolphin speak to us in a language we can understand, just like you did with the elephant, Bagarah."

In an instant, the dolphin's chattering turned into words. "I just had the strongest feeling that I was supposed to come here," the dolphin said in a high-pitched squeaky voice. "But I don't understand why? Nobody here except some mere humans."

"We're the reason you were sent here," Zonia said excitedly. Her voice startled the dolphin, who immediately disappeared under the water.

"Where did she go?" Shem asked.

Noah pulled thoughtfully at his gray beard. "I

think she wasn't expecting to hear a *mere human* speak to her."

"Come back, miss dolphin," Zonia called.

The choppy water sloshed as it rose and fell in the deep pool. They waited. Down deep at the bottom of the pool a bluish shadow appeared again. It swam round and round and slowly became more clear. Finally a shiny blue-gray head poked up above the water's surface just enough for two very large eyes to appear.

"It's okay," Zonia said. "We're friendly humans, and we really need your help."

The shiny head rose a little higher until the rounded bottle-like nose cleared the water. "Humans can talk?"

It was the same question Bagarah had asked, and Adam wondered if animals talk to each other all the time, but in a way people didn't understand?

Noah and Shem laughed. "It seems we speak the same language now. Praise be the Creator of All!"

"But how do I hear your speech now?" The dolphin asked. "I've never heard humans speak. Didn't know they were able to. They always only made strange noises like grunts and growls."

"It's a miracle," Adam said. "The Great King — you know Him as the Creator of All — made it happen."

The dolphin gave an excited chatter and rose half her body length out of the water as if standing on her tail. "I know the Creator. I was the first of my kind that He made!"

Adam's eyes got wide. "You were? Then that means you're over sixteen-hundred years old."

The dolphin made a scolding sound and narrowed her eyes at him. "Be careful, pup. It's not polite to talk about a ladies age."

"I'm sorry. My name is Adam, and this is my sister Zonia, and our friends, Mr. Noah and Mr. Shem."

"Pleased to make your acquaintances. I am," she spoke a word no one understood, but sounded a little like Gracy.

"Did you say Gracy?" Adam asked.

"Gracy is close enough. You probably can't pronounce it anyway," the dolphin said. "Why did Zonia say that you humans were the reason I was supposed to come here?" She looked around. "And by the way, where am I. From below this place looked like a human boat, but it is much larger than any boat I have ever seen."

Noah said, "It's a huge boat indeed, Miss Gracy. I built it because of the flood, to save the animals that breath air."

"I breath air," Gracy said, and she sounded a little put off that Noah hadn't noticed.

Noah laughed. "I should have said all the animals that breath air and live on land. You live in the seas. In case you haven't noticed, we have us a bit of a flood going on."

Gracy said she had noticed and that she has explored a few human villages which she had discovered, much to her surprise, to be completely under water now.

Adam said, "This flood covers the whole earth."

Zonia piped up, "And we lost something very important to the Creator of All and we need your help finding it."

"So that's why I'm here?"

Shem said, "We hoped that you could tell your friends, and they could tell their friends, and soon everyone who lives in the seas will help us find it."

"What did you lose?" Gracy asked.

Adam said, "A sack of apples. They fell into the sea. They belong to the Great King and we must find them. The Great King has given us the job of planting their seeds all throughout Gloriania and New Eden. That's the place where Zonia and I came from."

"I don't know what a sack of apples look like," Gracy said.

"I can show them to you," Adam said.

Gracy narrowed her eye in a confused look. "You said you lost them. How can you show them to me?"

"With this." Adam took the Dream Doodler from its holster. "I'll dream draw a picture of them for you. Okay?"

Gracy looked even more confused. "Okay . . . I guess."

Adam thought about the sack of apples, remembering how they looked. He closed his eyes, concentrating on the picture in his brain, waved the Dream Doodler in the air and pushed the Dream Draw button. A dream door portal opened and there the sack of apples were, exactly as he remembered them just before the two thieves stole them.

"Amazing," Gracy said, looking at the sack in the picture suspended in the air above her head. "Now I know what it is you lost."

The dream portal closed and the picture disappeared.

"Do you think you can find them for us?" Zonia asked.

"I don't know, but I'll try. I have lots of brothers and sisters and cousins. I'll tell them now."

Gracy dove under the water, her tail making a big splash, and then she was gone.

"Thank you," Zonia called, hoping Gracy had heard.

Noah said, "I hope the sea animals can find the lost apples. It would be fun to be part of the search."

Zonia looked at Adam with wide, hopeful eyes. "Could we somehow be part of the search?"

Adam thought a moment. "I think I have an idea."

Chapter 10

"WHAT IS IT?" NOAH ASKED WONDERINGLY AS HE peered at the strange boat that Adam had Dream Doodled in the air above the big table in the common room where everyone had gathered.

Adam said, "It's a special kind of boat called an EFTS -- an Exploretime Field Trip Submersible."

The boat was long and slender, with six big round windows along its hull. It bobbed upon the surface of the rough sea, but did not appear to be in any danger of sinking. The dream door remained open a few moments more, and then it snapped shut and the picture disappeared.

Adam said, "It's a submarine. There are many different kinds of submarines. In the Before Time they were sometimes used in wars, but in New Eden Time, we use them to explore and study the all the plants and animals that live under the water."

"Ah, an underwater boat!" Noah declared. "How very clever."

Zonia said, "Can we follow Gracy and all her brothers and sisters in it?" She knew very little about submarines. Children her age went to Pre-exploretime and didn't study things like submarines and airplanes and star gliders. Those subjects weren't taught until children got a little older and graduated to Exploretime, like Adam had a couple years ago.

Adam said, "Dolphins swim pretty fast, but the EFTS was built by Exploretime Lightons, and it's fast too. It has an underwater microphone so we'll be able to talk to Gracy and she can talk to us."

"Can we all come along in this wonderful craft?" Shem asked.

Noah said, "Some of us need to remain here. There are a lot of chores to do, and we barely have enough people to see to them as it is."

Adam said, "The Dream Doodler only works with people who were born in New Eden Time, but there is a trick we learned while visiting Grandfather Adam. I can Dream Draw some of you aboard the EFTS. It's kind of complicated because I've got to imagine you already there. It will be easier if only one or two come along."

Zonia said, "Mr. Noah must come along."

"I agree," Adam said. "And maybe one more." He looked to Noah. "Who else would you like to come with us?"

"Take me, take me," Kitah, blurted out. She was hopping up and down on her toes with excitement.

Noah laughed. "I think I would like Kitah to accompany us!"

"And Toby comes too," Zonia said. The big Siberian tiger rubbed against her side and purred. She treated him to a few seconds of scratching behind his orange ears.

Adam nodded. "Yes, Toby too."

Naamah said, "I'll pack a lunch," and she hurried off to the kitchen area.

Kitah, bubbling with excitement said, "Just let me grab my bag." Off she darted, down the long hallway and disappeared through a doorway.

"What about us? Can we go too?" Lester Groutt asked. "We were born in New Eden Time."

Noah said, "You mischief-makers have already caused enough problems. You will remain here and my sons will make sure you don't make any more trouble."

Ham took a coil of rope from the closet. "If you don't behave, I'll tie you to a post near the Behemoths. We haven't gotten around to cleaning their enclosure yet, and believe me, if it isn't cleaned every day the smell will make your brain numb."

Castor looked at Lester, his eyes wide with worry. "That sounds awful."

"Ah, shut up, bonehead. He's only saying that to

frighten us." Lester pushed out his chest and crossed his arms belligerently.

But no one in the gathering room was smiling. Feeling their hot stares on him, Lester shrank back in his chair and looked kind of worried himself.

"What else will we need to take with us?" Noah asked Adam.

"Everything we'll need is already in the EFTS."

"I hope Gracy and her family and friends find the apples soon," Zonia said. "I feel like we've been away from home an awful long time, and I miss mom and dad." She hugged Toby's neck.

"I'm back," Kitah called, bounding into the gathering room, her face glowing with excitement. She had wound up her long hair into a bright green cap. Over her shoulder hung a huge bag woven from red, gold, and blue thread. "Let go!"

Naamah handed Kitah a large wicker basket. "It's all I have on hand, but it should be enough to feed the four — err, the *five* of you," she added seeing Toby. "Now what do I have that a tiger would like to eat."

"At home we feed Toby fruitons and catvage, but I don't guess you would have any of that here." Adam scrunched his eye together suddenly remembering something. "Wait, mom packed a lunch for us too. Maybe she . . ."

He grabbed the backpack from the corner where Zonia had set it down earlier. "*YES!*" He unwrapped a big, juicy fruiton and tossed it into the air just like he'd seen his dad do a hundred times before. Toby leaped for it, catching it in his teeth, swallowing it down in one gulp.

"There's catvage in here too, and some sandwiches." Adam slung the backpack over his shoulder. "Between us, we'll have plenty to eat, Mrs. Noah."

"We're ready then," Noah said. "What do we do now?"

"You don't have to do a thing. I'll take care of it. Ready?"

"Ready," each of them said.

Adam took the Dream Doodler from its holster and closed his eyes, thinking about the EFTS, remembering exactly how it looked, only this time he imagined Noah and Kitah sitting in the seats that lined up in a row alongside the large round windows. With that picture sharply in his brain, he waved the Dream Doodler in the air and pressed the Dream Draw button.

In a flash Kitah and Noah disappeared.

Naamah, Seth, Japheth, Ham, Majiah, and Desmorah gave startled gasp. But then the dream portal opened before their eyes. Beyond the portal, Noah and Kitah were sitting safely inside the EFTS just as Adam had imagined them.

"Quick, before the portal closes," Zonia said. She grabbed a handful of Toby's orange fur and they stepped through the portal into the Dream

Draw picture — into the EFTS submarine — and the portal closed behind them.

* * *

LESTER WAITED until Noah's sons weren't watching and busy elsewhere doing Ark chores. Then he leaned close to Castor and whispered, "We can still make our plan work."

"W-what plan is that? Remind me."

"You bonehead! Don't you remember we're going to get those apples back and give them to the Evols. The Evols will be so happy, they're bound to reward us."

"Oh, yeah. I remember now." Castor looked a little confused, which is how Castor often looked.

"What's wrong now?" Lester asked impatiently.

"W-well, how we going to get the apples back? And when we do, how do we tell the Evols we have them? And, if Adam Beam ever finds out, we'll never get back home."

"Bonehead. Don't try to figure it out. Let me do the thinking. All you have to do is follow me. Okay?"

Castor worked this over in his brain a while, and then he gave a big smile. "Gee, that was easy."

Lester rolled his eyes and stood from the chair and strolled toward the door. Ham stood just outside it, leaning against a post, the coil of rope in his hand.

"Where do you think you're going?"

Lester looked around innocently. "Me? I'm not going anywhere. This is a really big boat. I've heard stories about Noah's Ark all my life, and now that I'm actually on it, well, I thought it might be interesting to see what it really looks like."

Ham relaxed a little. "I guess it won't hurt for you to look around the ship some. I'll stroll along with you, just so you don't get hurt."

"That's great," Lester said. He figured if he acted harmless, Ham would drop his guard long enough for him to make his move. In any case, it didn't hurt to explore a little and get a feel for the lay of the land, so to speak.

"How long did it take to build it?"

Ham thought a moment. "In the beginning we spent a lot of time drawing up proper plans and buying tools and the wood and pitch. There were special pieces that had to be made; gas and water pipes, iron hangers and brackets. The Tubal-cain Company built most of those for us. Once we had everything we needed and a plot of land large enough to build it on, we hired a crew of workmen to do the actual building. All in all, it took about ten years to build."

"It must have cost a lot of money." Lester thought Noah and his family were really wealthy. He kept an eye out for anything small and valuable that he could hide in his pocket and sell later.

"Indeed it did, but the Creator of All supplied

the money. Whenever we needed something, someone would come forward and provide it. And that was peculiar seeing as my father was not well liked."

"Why wasn't he liked?" Lester didn't have many friends, except for Castor, and that bothered him a little. He didn't like being alone.

Ham said, "Pop spent over a hundred years preaching of the coming flood and the people's need to repent. They only laughed at him. They said he was crazy building a boat on dry land. And they didn't repent."

"How did you collect all the animals?" Lester recognized many of them, but couldn't remember their names. He'd been taught their names once, when he attended Exploretime. His teacher had told his class that many of the animals later become extinct, which meant they were no long alive, but Lester couldn't be bothered filling his head with useless information. After the Trouble Times were over, the Great King re-created all the extinct animals. In New Eden Time nothing was extinct anymore.

"We didn't have to gather them. The Creator of All sent them to us when it was time. That's how we knew the end was near." Ham looked at Lester and gave a half-grin. "And that was a clue to all those people who didn't believe pop. When the animals began arriving, two by two, some people started getting worried. Even so, they weren't ready to admit pop was right. It wasn't until The Creator of All sealed us inside here and the rain began to fall that the people realized their mistake. By then it was too late." He shook his head and looked sad. "They are all gone now. We are all that is left of mankind."

But by now Lester had lost interest in what Ham was saying. His thoughts turned back to figuring out how he could get the apples from Adam Beam and give them to the Evols. Shem had been hurt, and Adam and the others suspected the Evols had been responsible. Maybe the Evols were already here, aboard Noah's Ark?

"What's so funny?" Ham asked him.

Lester was grinning at that thought. He quickly put on a straight face. "Nothin's funny. What can be funny about living in a boat with a few thousand smelly animals."

Ham nodded. "The smell could be a lot worse if we didn't have the deep pool moving air in and out of the ship." He grinned. "Now that you and your friend have arrived, we had two more workers to help us clean up the place."

Ham stopped in front of a big pen with two hippopotami munching away at grass-like stalks in a tub of water. "Here you go." He picked up a large shovel leaning against the pen.

Lester's eyes got big. "What am I supposed to do with that?"

Ham pointed at a smelly pile with flies buzzing

around it. "Use *this* to shovel *that* into that trough over there, and I'll wash it down the chute with this hose. When we're done we'll give those two a bath. They really love to be sprayed down."

Lester crossed his arms. "I won't do it."

"Won't you?" Ham turned the hose toward Lester and grabbed a big bronze lever. "Maybe you'd like a bath too."

"You wouldn't dare."

"Want to find out?"

Scared that Ham was going to hose him down, Lester grabbed the shovel. Holding his nose, he slipped between the rails of the pen and got to work on the unpleasant job.

Chapter 11

THE LITTLE SUBMARINE LEAPED ABOUT UPON THE surface of the stormy sea like a toothpick in a washing machine. Adam grasped the back of one of the seats to keep from falling. He held Zonia's hand tightly while Zonia held onto a fistful of orange fur. Toby, having four legs instead of two, easily kept his balance. Adam had *imagined* Noah and Kitah already buckled into seats before he Dream Drew them, and there they were, safe and secure.

"Everyone all right?" Adam asked. Beyond the row of big round windows dark roiling clouds filled a gloomy sky. Sea water pounded the window as the submarine plunged back and forth.

Kitah's face looked pale. "I thought I was used to rough seas. Our ship feels like it's sailing on smooth water compared to this."

"Our ship is so much larger," Noah said, "its size helps smooth out the rough waves."

Adam pulled himself along to the front of the submarine and slid in the pilot's seat behind the controls. Zonia sat in the co-pilot's seat and quickly fastened her seatbelt. Toby sat on the floor behind them, his front feet splayed to help him keep his balance.

"It will be a lot smoother once we're underwater." Adam studied the controls, remembering the last time he had operated an EFTS at Explortime Ocean Discovery Camp earlier that year. It all came back to him in a flash. He turned a switch, pushed a lever and rotated a small wheel-like valve at his side.

The EFTS started forward, fighting against the mighty waves. Adam gripped the yoke — the main control that looked a little like a steering wheel — and pushed it forward. The submarine's nose tilted downward and in a minute they were far below the angry sea. The water was much smoother down here, although Adam felt a strong current pushing at the EFTS rudder.

Kitah gave a large sigh of relief. "I thought I might get sea sick. This is better."

Noah peered out the windows and frowned. "I wish I could see better." The water was dark because there was no sunlight to pierce the thick clouds above. "How will we ever know where Gracy is, or see the sack of apples once she finds them?"

Adam searched the control panel for the switch

marked *Spotlights*. "This ought to help." Powerful underwater lights snapped on, lighting up the water a bright as daylight on a sunny day.

"Amazing technology you have in New Eden Time," Noah said.

"We have many even more amazing things. The Brightons and Lightons can carry us in star gliders to any planet in the solar system, and even the stars, if we want to go there."

Noah struggled to comprehend it all. "I should like to visit you in New Eden Time someday."

"You will," Zonia piped up. "You live there now. You're one of the Brightons."

"I am? Have we met in your New Eden Time?"

"No, not yet, but we will someday."

Kitah had her nose to one of the big round windows. "So many beautiful fish. Their colors are amazing, and they give off flashed of light like they were made of stained glass."

Adam said, "In Exploretime we learned that those lights are called bioluminescence."

Kitah said, "The fish seem upset, schooling in great circles as if they don't know where to go."

Noah said, "It's this flood. Even though they live under the water, they sense something terrible is happening to the world."

Adam said, "I'm going to try to contact Gracy." He turned on the underwater microphone. "Calling Gracy, calling Gracy. This is Adam Beam."

Adam's words traveled through the water from

powerful underwater speakers. Even so, they sounded muffled through the submarine's hull, as if he was speaking into a wad of cotton.

"If she's a long way off will she be able to hear you?" Kitah asked.

Adam remembered his Exploretime lessons on dolphins. "Dolphins are like whales. They have excellent hearing. I'll try again. Adam calling Gracy. Can you hear me?"

A few moments later Gracy's high-pitched dolphin voice chattered in the speakers over Adam's head.

"There she is," Noah announced pointing at a distant blue-gray shape darting swiftly toward the EFTS.

Gracy shot past the submarine, looking wary. Shying away from the long white submarine, she circled it twice, peering into every window as she did. "Adam Beam. Is that you? Why are you inside that large fish? Have you been eaten?"

Zonia laughed.

Adam spoke into the microphone. "Hi Gracy. Yes, it's I. We're not inside a fish. We're inside a submarine, a special kind of boat that can travel underwater."

"I can tell it is not alive, but I have never seen anything like it before."

"Have you started searching for the sack of apples?" Adam asked.

"I told my brothers and sisters and friends —

everyone of our kind that I could find. And they are telling all their friends too. Soon there will be thousands of sea swimmers looking for the lost apples. As soon as I told them the apples belong to the Creator of All, everyone was excited to help."

Gracy circled around the submarine as she spoke, peeking inside from different viewing windows. "It's a good hunt," she continued. "It will help us sea swimmers not to worry too much about the disturbance. None of us understands what has happened to our world, but we know it can't be good."

Noah said, "It is not good at all. Mankind has not obeyed the Creator and has been very unkind to their brothers and sisters. Worse yet, they have allowed evil spirits to influence them. What is happening to the world now is the Creator's punishment for mankind's evil deeds."

"In that case, I am very happy I am not a man kind, but a fin kind." Gracy left, promising to return as soon as she had any news to report.

Adam piloted the submarine deeper and deeper, and soon the bottom was visible. Undersea earthquakes and bursting fountains of water stirred up the mud making the water murky. The submarine's powerful search lights pierced the gloom and revealed the muddy sea floor and hundreds of different kinds of sea creatures. Strong currents shaped large ripples in the sea floor that appeared to snake along the mud.

Something like a landslide of mud rushed toward the submarine.

Quickly Adam steered away from it and pushed a lever for more speed.

"That was close," Zonia said looking over her shoulder at the churning brown cloud of silt behind them.

"That was a part of my world washing away," Noah said in a sad voice. "Everything we once knew has disappeared. I fear that when we step off the ark, we won't recognize anything."

Recalling his Exploretime lessons, Adam said, "It will all be different, Mr. Noah. We learned that during the flood the land broke apart into many pieces and moved across the earth. That's how the continents were formed."

"What are continents?" Kitah asked.

"Large chunks of land, usually separated by oceans but sometimes connected by narrow pieces of land," Adam told them.

"Like islands?" She asked.

"Sort of like islands, only much, much larger."

A large fish with big eyes and a mouth that opened and closed and opened and closed swam close to look them over. Toby bounded to one of the windows, put his paws on its rim and stared back at the fish. The fish quickly veered away.

Kitah laughed and stroked Toby's furry head. "That old fish didn't like the sight of a ferocious tiger."

Zonia said, "Ferocious like a kitten."

Everyone laughed.

Adam spied a group of dolphins. A group of dolphins is called a pod, and this pod was at the farthest reaches of the submarines spotlights. Looking uncertain as to what they ought to be doing, they swam about poking their noses here and there.

Adam pointed out the forward window. "I think that's Gracy and her friends."

Noah watched them a moment and then shook his head. "They'll never find the apples searching in such a haphazard way. They need someone to command them."

Adam said, "Sort of like how an admiral commands a navy?"

"Exactly, my young friend."

Adam said, "I wouldn't know how to tell them to search, but I'll bet you could do it, Mr. Noah."

Noah pulled thoughtfully at his gray beard and got a faraway look in his eyes as if remembering something. "Well, I did do a lot of sailing in my younger days. I commanded a group of explorers and we sailed far south to the land of Morgseth where my mother and father once lived. But I haven't commanded sailing men for a very long time. Not for at least two hundred years before the Creator of All warned me about the coming flood and instructed me to build this ship."

Zonia said, "You haven't forgotten how to be an admiral, have you?"

Noah chuckled. "I was never an admiral, young lady. And no, I haven't forgotten how to lead men."

Adam handed Noah the microphone. "They're dolphins, not men, but they're your navy to command."

Noah looked at the device, a little puzzled. Adam realized Noah had never seen a microphone before. "You just hold down that button there on the side and talk into it."

He did, cautious at first, and looked a bit startled hearing his own words boom out into the water. "Attention. Calling all dolphins and whales." He glanced over at Adam and grinned. He pressed the talk button again. "This is Admiral Noah. I need all whales and dolphins to assemble here."

A great number of underwater animals began arriving. They came from every direction and gathered around the submarine.

Kitah said, "I had no idea the seas contained so many fish."

"They really do look like fish," Zonia said, "but I learned that dolphins and whales aren't fish at all. They're mammals. They have hair, and nurse their babies like human mothers."

"And they breath air just like we do," Adam added. "Only, they can hold their breath a lot longer."

Kitah said, "I can hold my breath a long time, but not as long as these animals."

Zonia laughed. "My cheeks would burst if I tried!"

For the next few minutes Noah's great navy grew larger and larger around the little Exploretime submarine. Noah clicked on the microphone again.

"Thank you for coming here. We have an important mission to accomplish. We must find the sack of apples that belong to the Creator of All, and was lost at sea. The area to search is very large, but there are many of you to do the searching."

Noah explained how they were to gather in small pods. Each pod was to select a commander and then swim in a grid pattern across the seafloor. Noah assigned Gracy to be his official liaison.

Zonia gave Adam a puzzled look. "What's a liaison?"

"A liaison is like a messenger. Gracy will carry messages back and forth so that Admiral Noah will be kept informed on how well his navy is searching."

"Oh. Like the Lightons are messengers for the Great King."

The dolphins and whales immediately followed Admiral Noah's orders. They organized themselves in pods and began searching for the lost sack of apples. Gracy remained near the submarine. She said, "I'll check on each group and keep you informed."

"Thank you, Gracy," Noah said into the microphone.

She started away. Adam pushed a lever forward and the EFLS moved ahead.

Toby put his paws of the edge of one of the windows and watched the dolphins and whales. Instead of swimming in endless circles, they now swam in a nice, organized search patterns.

Admiral Noah said, "Now we'll get somewhere." He stood very straight with his back arched and looked every bit the image of a ship's commander. "We ought to have those apples back shortly."

The submarine lurched violently and titled steeply to one side. Everyone grabbed something to keep from being thrown off their feet. Admiral Noah nearly tumbled onto Kitah's lap. Toby sprawled across one of the big, round window.

"What was that?" Zonia cried, holding tight.

Adam struggled with the controls to bring the submarine back upright. Luckily his seat belt had held him safely in place. Beyond the porthole the seafloor had been ripped wide open and a geyser of steaming water was shooting up, as if from a hose under enormous pressure.

He quickly steered away from the violent water. "That must be one of the fountains of the deep that the Bible talks about." Adam stared at the terrifying sight. "Good thing for us we weren't directly over that when it erupted."

Admiral Noah said, "The Creator of All is watching over us."

"Amen," Zonia said softly.

"I'm getting scared now," Kitah said. Her face looked pale. Toby nuzzled close to her as if trying to reassure her.

The crack in the sea floor grew wider and went zigzagging along.

The EFTS powerful motors sped them away from that fountain of the deep and the water cleared a little.

Zonia pointed out the window. "There they are."

The dolphins and whales were still swimming in straight lines, back and forth.

Chapter 12

LESTER GROUTT WAS ALMOST TOO TIRED TO DRAG himself back to the main room with the big table. His clothes were grimy, his hands filthy, and he smelled so awful that everyone groaned when he came in.

Ham followed several paces behind him, wearing a grin.

All Lester wanted to do was collapse and go to sleep. He aimed his heavy feet toward the nearest chair, but before he could sit, Mrs. Noah said, "First things first, young man." She crooked a finger for him to follow her down the hallway and into a room with a big bath tub and rows of fluffy cotton towels.

Mrs. Noah filled the tub with hot water and sprinkled soap flakes into it. "Get out of those filthy clothes and chuck them into the hallway. I'll throw them into the automatic scrubber." She stepped out of the room and closed the door.

Lester eagerly eyed the tub. He was happy to sink into the soapy water and scrub off all the filth. The soap smelled strawberries and bananas. The tub was so relaxing, he almost fell asleep, but he shook himself awake at the creak of the door opening and then closing. When he looked, his clothes were laying in a neat pile upon a little shelf.

"That was quick!" he said to himself, wondering what sort of washing machine could clean and dry his clothes in what had to have been less than twenty minutes.

Lester climbed out of the tub and dried himself with one of the towels. The bathtub automatically swished the dirty water away, and a strong stream of clean water cascaded down the sides, washing all the leftover grime down the drain.

His clothes were soft and still warm from the drying. He dressed and stepped back out into the hallway. He didn't feel so tired anymore as he padded back to the gathering room in stocking feet. The big table was set out with a clean tablecloth, plates, knives, forks, and crystal glasses that took on different colors depending on which way the light caught them.

Mrs. Noah, Desmorah, and Majiah busily prepared dinner. Shem carried a big platter of steaming vegetables and set it in the middle of the table.

Ham and Japheth blessed the food with a prayer that sounded like choral speaking and then everyone filled their plates. Lester didn't recognize all the vegetables, but they were delicious and he was hungry.

By the way Castor gobbled down his food, he must have been hungry too.

Afterward, Ham helped clear the table. Shem said to Japheth, "Let's go down and have another look at the broken shelf. Maybe we can fix it and finish cleaning up that mess?"

Lester's ears perked up with interest. He caught Castor's eye and hitched his head toward the two brothers as they left the room. Castor gave him a blank stare.

"Let's follow them," Lester whispered.

"W-why?" Castor asked.

Lester rolled his eyes disgustedly. "You bone-head! That broken shelf is where the Evols were. They might still be down there."

Castor's eyes slowly widened as understanding seeped reluctantly into his brain.

Lester whispered, "No one is watching us now. Let's go."

Quietly the two fellows pushed back their chairs and tiptoed unseen out the doorway. Ham and Japheth were up ahead, just starting down the long ramp. At the bottom they crossed a brightly lit deck filled with large pens. Here were elephants and huge oxes, giraffes and baby dinosaurs. Soon they left the pens behind and the overhead lights grew further and further apart. The place became gloomy as piles of boxes and rows of barrels replaced the animals.

Lester and Castor hid behind some barrels watching Noah's sons examining the big shelf. Nearby was the crushed vehicle that had saved Shem's life.

"W-what are they doing. I can't see." Castor crawled around the barrel for a better look.

Lester hit Castor over the head with his cap. "Shush, bonehead. They'll hear you. They're just cleaning up the mess, that's all."

Noah's sons sorted through the stuff that had fallen across the floor, separating it into neat piles off to one side. When they had finished, they examined the fallen shelf, deciding what to do with it.

"It's too heavy to lift without the winch," Japheth said.

Ham thought a moment. "That's a lot of work We'd have to dig it out of the long-term storage rooms and haul it up from down below."

Japheth thought a moment and then shook his head. "That *is* a lot of work. We have plenty of room aboard the ship, why don't we just move all this stuff out of the way and take the shelf apart? We can stack the wood aside to use later to build our new homes when we finally leave here and step out onto dry land again."

"Good idea. Let's get busy."

Castor crept around the barrel for a better look

and tipped over a small can at his elbow. Lester grimaced. "Stop moving around, bonehead!"

But Japheth and Ham were so busy cleaning up around the shelf, they didn't hear.

Lester and Castor waited. Castor became impatient and kept fidgeting, trying to peek out. Lester thought he would have to sit on his friend to keep him in place.

A long, torturous hour passed. "I'm hungry," Castor complained.

"You just ate," Bonehead.

"So? I get hungry not doing nothin'," Castor said, his voice pouty, a little louder than a whisper.

Lester whacked him over the head again with his cap.

"Well, that does it." Ham brushed his hands together. The two brothers stood back and looked at the neat pile of supplies they had made.

"I'm tired," Japheth said. "We can finish up here tomorrow."

"I'm for that. Hey, maybe there is some of that cake left? Let's go see." The two of them started away.

"C-cake," Castor moaned and started crawling out from behind the barrel.

Lester grabbed him by the cuff of his pants. "Where do you think you're going?"

"I want some cake too."

"All you think about is your stomach! Now that they are gone, we can try to find those Evols.

"A-are you sure you want to, Lester? Evols are scary."

"Maybe a little, but they want those apples, and if we can get them, the Evols will give us gold."

"What if they don't?"

Lester frowned. He hadn't thought about that. "Well, we'll just make sure they do." He didn't know how to force an Evol to do anything, but he was never one to let minor details get in his way.

* * *

FOR THE NEXT several hours Adam piloted the EFTS alongside the teams of dolphins and whales searching the seafloor for the lost sack of apples.

Gracy turned out to be an excellent liaison, reporting back to them whenever a search team had spotted something looking like a sack of apples. And each time Adam expertly steered the little submarine to the spot, but so far every discovery had turned out to be something different. One time a whale discovered an old tent that had sunk to the bottom. Another time a dolphin discovered a burlap sack. When Adam used the sub's remote grabbers to pick it up, the sack turned out to contain only a bunch of rusty nails.

"I'm getting hungry," Kitah said after a while. "Anybody else want to eat?"

"Yes, yes," they cried, and even Toby a long,

pitiful yowl of hunger. Everybody laughed and soon they were all munching on sandwiches.

"This is like having a picnic at the bottom of the sea!" Zonia said. Toby purred loudly and contentedly at her side, eating the catvage Mrs. Beam had packed with their lunch.

"Adam Bean, Adam Beam," Gracy's voice screeched over the loudspeaker.

Adam grabbed the microphone. "Hi Gracy. What news do you bring?"

She gave a high-pitched dolphin laugh, which really wasn't a laugh at all. It was just the way dolphins express their excitement.

"I think the sack of apples has been found this time."

"Great, Gracy. Where are they?"

She swam near the window and looked in at them. "It's a long way from here, and we must hurry. The sea bottom is splitting open again and scalding hot water is beginning to bubble up from the deep's cracks."

Admiral Noah asked for the microphone. "Lead the way, Gracy. We'll follow you as fast as we can." He glanced at Adam. "How fast can we go?"

"I don't know, sir, but I'll give it all we've got."

Gracy turned and darted away. "Hold on," Adam said to his crew, pushing the lever all the way forward. The little submarine surged ahead, its motors whirring loudly. Even so, Gracy pulled ahead of them. The Great King had designed dolphins to be fast and graceful swimmers, and although the Lightons had built the EFTS, the little submarine was no match for a dolphin in a great hurry.

Kitah pointed out the window at the seafloor speeding past. "Look at that!" A crack had opened up and was growing wider by the second.

"Now I'm getting a little scared," Zonia said, gripping the arm of her chair tighter.

"Me too," Adam admitted.

The crack widened as they went along. Gracy veered off to the side of it because the water bubbling from the crack was boiling hot, like water in a pot on a stove top. More frightening still, when they peered deep down into the bottom of the crack they saw red-hot lava churning and glowing like burning coals, rising higher and higher.

"I can feel the heat," Admiral Noah said in a worried voice. He put his hand against one of the windows. "The flood judgment is ripping our earth apart."

Adam wondered if the heat might damage the EFTS? He steered away from the crack and, looking around, realized he could no longer see Gracy. "Where did she go?" He turned in his seat to peer out each of the many windows.

Admiral Noah grabbed the microphone and pressed the talk button. "Gracy, where are you?"

Kitah said, "The last time I saw her, she was

swimming in that direction." She pointed out the window.

Zonia said, "We might be going in the wrong direction."

"We'll find her," Adam said, trying to sound confident, but he was also worried they had become lost.

And then they Gracy's high pitch squeals came loudly over the speakers.

"There she is!" Zoina pointed upward.

Gracy was swimming straight down at them.

Admiral Noah said, "Where did you go, Gracy?"

"I had to swim to the surface for a breath of air. I've been under water an awful long time. And talking uses up my air faster." She turned on her tail and shot off again, her voice growing distant as she sped away. "This way."

In a few more minutes a great gathering of sea creatures came into sight.

"That must be the place," Adam said steering the submarine toward them.

"I hope not." Kitah's voice was strangely tight. She pointed. "Look at that!"

Adam's chest squeezed with fear. The great, boiling volcanic crack was zigzagging across the sea floor, moving more or less in the direction of the place where the apples were! "Oh no! We have to hurry."

The gathering of dolphins and whales moved

aside as the submarine arrived. "Is that the sack of apples, Adam Beam?" Gracy swam around and round the sack that was half buried in the mud.

"That's it!" Adam glanced out the window at the zigzagging crack racing closer. "We've got to hurry. Swim aside and I'll use the EFTS's remote grabbers to pick it up."

He moved the submarine in closer and switched over to the grabber control. It looked like an old fashion joy stick children used to play games with in the time before New Eden Time. Mrs. Levin, his Exploretime teacher, had taught a lesson on the games children used to play in the Before Time.

Zonia's eyes were big and round as the fearsome crack raced along the bottom getting ever closer. "Hurry Adam."

Adam tried to hurry, but he had to maneuver the EFTS in close with one hand and operate the grabber control with the other. He extended the grabber arm and opened the mechanical claw. The claw reached for the sack of apples. It opened and . . .

The crack reached the sack first. The ground crumbled away and the sack of Adam's Apples slid into the fiery abyss.

Kitah and Admiral Noah groaned.

"We lost them," Zonia cried.

"No wait!" Admiral Noah pointed as a blue-gray flash streaked past the window and shot down into the boiling abyss.

Kitah gasped. "That's Gracy!" Sudden fear tightened her face. "How will she survive?"

No one could speak a word. Every eye had fixed upon the place where the apples and Gracy had disappeared. The seconds stretched out. They felt like hours to Adam Beam. And then Gracy reappeared. She held the sack in her mouth as she struggled out of the out of the fearsome crack of doom. Something was wrong. She swam weakly away from the deadly fissure and then turned onto her side and sank to the bottom.

Admiral Noah said, "She's hurt."

"What can we do?" Kitah asked.

Adam drove the submarine to where Gracy had fallen and grabbed the microphone. "Gracy, can you hear me? Gracy?"

The brave dolphin didn't say a word.

Chapter 13

CASTOR AND LESTER CREPT FROM THEIR HIDING place behind the big barrel and stood where Japheth and Ham had just cleared up the mess. The huge shelf still lay across the floor on top of a little yellow and green. Lester looked up into the dark rafters. The place felt a little spooky, and a shiver ticked his spine.

Castor whispered, "I-I wish there was more light here."

Lester did too, but he pretended to be brave. "Sissy." He puffed out his chest. "Follow me."

They crept around the shelf and tiptoed down a long aisle. Mountains of dark supplies and strange-looking machines crouched in the shadows on either side. "Hello." Lester said weakly, a tremble in his voice. He cleared his throat and said a little more boldly, "Hello? Calling all Evols. Can you hear me?"

"I don't think they hear you. L-let's go back upstairs and have some cake." Castor turned.

Lester whacked him on the head with his cap.

"Ouch!"

"Shut up and let me think. I know!" Lester cleared his throat again and timidly raised his voice. "If you Evols want those apples back, I can get them for you." He paused and listened, looking around.

Castor gave a gasp and pointed at a dark valley between two mountains of stuff. Three pair of yellow eyes glowed in the darkness. They seemed to float in the air as they moved toward the two thieves. Lester took in a deep breath and tried not to be frightened. He'd had never seen Evols before, and the sight of them was startling.

Three creatures emerged from the shadows into the dim light of the aisle. They wore long black robes with black hoods over their heads so that only their sickly yellow eyes were visible. Lester didn't see any feet beneath the robes. They floated just above the floor

"Who are you and why have you summoned us," an Evol with a high, cackling voice asked. His long bony finger stretched out from the black sleeve.

Lester grabbed Castor's arm and half stepped behind his taller friend. "I'm Lester Mudd. And-and I hear that you want Adam's Apples."

"Ah, so that's it? Yes, His Magnificence desires

the apples. They were stolen from him by some nasty children. He was very angry."

Castor squirmed out of Lester's grip and crouched behind his shorter, fatter friend. But Lester was feeling braver now. "I might be able to get them for His Magnificence."

"Why would you do this?" the second Evol asked, his voice sounding like screechy fingernails scratching across a chalk board.

"Because I want a reward."

"What reward do you seek?" asked the third Evol in a high brittle voice like cold wind rattling winter branches.

"Gold," Lester said. "Lots and lots of gold."

Cackling laughter filled the gloomy depths of the Ark. One of the Evols drifter closer to Lester. "You do not seek very much, do you?" If there was a face inside the hood, Lester couldn't see it. And if an arm was attached to the bony hand and finger that wavered in front of his nose, he couldn't see that either.

Lester's courage was melting quickly. "Well, that's what I want. Is it a deal?"

"A deal?" The brittle-voice one asked. They chuckled among themselves. "You bring the apples to us and we will give you your gold." The Evols drifted back into the darkness.

Lester drew in a sharp breath, turned and fled from the darkness back into the light. Castor was right behind him. Up the ramp they flew and didn't stop running until they screeched to a halt back to the common room. Only Mrs. Noah was there, when they arrived. She looked up and smiled.

"Where have you two been?"

"Oh, nowhere," Lester managed to say, breathing hard. "Just looking at the animals. Ain't that right, Castor?"

Castor gulped a couple times and nodded, still too frightened to say anything.

* * *

ADAM MOVED the submarine in as close as he could to the brave, fallen dolphin.

"Gracy is hurt," Zonia said. "We have to help her!"

Adam gently nudged Gracy with the mechanical arm. Her eyes moved a little, but that was all. She'd been too badly injured by the scalding water to move.

Admiral Noah said, "Dolphins are air-breathing animals. If she doesn't wake up soon, she will drown."

"Oh no!" Kitah cried. "Whatever shall we do?"

"We need to get her to the surface," Admiral Noah said.

"How?" Zonia asked.

"I have an idea." Adam turned back to the

controls and moved a lever. A motor rumbled inside the submarine and four little legs extended from its bottom. The submarine gave a gentle thump as it settled down on the seafloor next to Gracy.

Zonia asked, "What's the plan, Adam?"

"I'm going to dream draw Gracy inside a crystal dome like the one at the Creation Botanical Gardens back home." He pulled the Dream Doodler from its holster and closed his eyes, remembering the large glass dome in Glorainia where all kinds of flowers grow, and birds fly and water tumbles down pretty rock formations. He pictured the dome on the seafloor with Gracy and the Submarine inside it. Waving the Dream Doodler in the air, he pressed the Dream Draw button.

"By Methuselah's beard!" Admiral Noah exclaimed, his nose pressed against one of the submarines large viewing windows. "Is there no limits to the wonders your Dream Doodler can do?"

Adam shoved it back into its holster. "I don't think so, not when it has the blessings of the Great King. Come on."

He opened the hatch in the ceiling and they climbed the ladder out onto the top of the submarine. Toby had a hard time climbing the ladder so instead he crouched and leaped, clearing the hatch with ease and landing on the railed platform with the others.

Zonia hugged Toby's orange, furry neck. "I feel safer with you at my side, Toby."

The great Siberian Tiger nuzzled his nose into her side and somehow, like always, managed to get his ear under her hand, purring loudly as she scratched it.

Quickly they climbed another ladder down to the seafloor. Toby leaped after them.

"Yuck," Zonia said as her shoes sank into the mud up to her ankles. "You should have dream doodled a dry floor, Adam."

He lifted one foot and looked at the globs of mud dripping from it. "I'm sorry. I didn't think about that."

They went to Gracy, their shoes making a sucking sound with each step. Toby lifted and shook the mud off of each paw as he went. The short trip was not easy.

Gracy looked really sick, and confused. "Don't worry," Zonia said, "we'll take care of you."

"She's been boiled," Admiral Noah observed.

Kitah fell to her knees, paying no attention to the mud. She started to gently touch the smooth skin on Gracy's head, but then stopped, not wanting to hurt the dolphin anymore than she already was. "Can you hear us, dear?"

Gracy made a weak dolphin squeal and rolled one eye toward Kitah.

Adam's thoughts raced. What might they be

able to do to help the poor dolphin? "What medicine would make her better?" he asked.

Admiral Noah said, "There is only one thing I know of, and that's the tree of healing. But it only grew inside the Creator's Garden, which he had planted east of Eden. Unfortunately, the Garden no longer exists. This flood has seen to that. And even when it did, men were forbidden to go there, except one or two."

"How do you know about this healing tree?" Adam asked.

"Well, you see, many, many years after Father Adam was told he and Mother Eve had to leave the Garden, my mother was allowed inside the Garden. And I was . . ." He broke off in mid sentence as if what he was about to reveal was something he probably should not talk about.

"Zonia and I can go there," Adam said at once. "The Dream Doodler will take us anywhere, as long as I can imagine it."

Admiral Noah's eyes got big. "Can we go all with you?"

"Well . . . maybe. The Dream Doodler only works for people who were born in New Eden Time. The only way for it to work with you is for me to imagine you already there. Like how I was able to get you into the EFTS submarine."

"But you can do it?" Admiral Noah asked excitedly.

Zonia said, "If you all come with us, who will

stay here with Gracy? She'll be frightened all by herself."

"I will," Kitah volunteered. "I'll stay here and keep her company."

"It won't seem like we were gone any time at all," Adam reassured her. He looked at Admiral Noah, "I still don't know what the Garden looks like, and if I don't get it exactly right, we'll end up in the wrong place."

"I have a picture," Noah said.

"Where?"

"In the library, on board the ship."

Adam pulled the Dream Doodler from its holster and shut his eyes, imagining the large common room with the big table where the family ate their meals. When he had a clear picture of it inside his head, he imagined Noah standing by the table, and waved the Dream Doodler, pressing the Dream Draw button. As the dream door portal opened in the air Noah blinked out of sight and appeared inside the drawing, standing right next to the table exactly as Adam imagined him.

Dream Doors always amazed Adam. A warm feeling of love filled his heart. The Great King who made them possible was most wonderful and glorious person in the whole universe. The whole creation! After all, the Great King had made everything!

"Quickly," Zonia said, "before the dream door

closes." She jumped through the portal into the picture, and Toby leaped after her."

"We'll be right back," Adam told Kitah. He spied the sack of apples lying near Gracy. "I better take these." He grabbed up the sack and jumped through the portal too.

Mrs. Noah had a startled look on her face when Adam's feet landed with a thump on the common room's floor. "My! You all come and go in such a dramatic way."

Zonia giggled. "You ought to see the Wind Way."

"What's the Wind Way?" she asked.

"It's how people in Gloriainia travel from place to place in New Eden Time. You'll see it someday."

"I'm sure I'll look forward to that," Mrs. Noah said, sounding like she really wasn't all that certain that she would.

Ham said, "I'm anxious to see New Eden. It sounds like a wonderful place to live."

"It is," Adam and Zonia said at the same time.

Just then Lester and Castor ran into the room. They skidded to a halt, breathing hard. They each wore a frightened look on their faces.

"What have you two been up to?" Shem demanded. "Do I have to tie you up to keep you in one place and out of trouble?"

Lester stammered. "We were just exploring, that's all. Ain't that right, Castor?"

Castor couldn't seem to speak. His eyes were

stretched wide with the look of terror in them. He glanced around as if afraid something would leap from a dark corner and attack him.

Lester whipped off his cap and smacked Castor on the head. "I said, 'ain't that right."

Castor winced and rubbed his head. "Yeah, that's right."

Admiral Noah studied them suspiciously. "Why the frightened looks?"

"Frightened?" Lester laughed nervously. "We were just down looking at the dinosaurs with those long horns. One of them tried to stab us through the rails."

"Dinosaur?" Admiral Noah asked. "What's a dinosaur?"

"You know, those really BIG animals?"

"I think he means a three-point," Japheth told his father. "They must have different names for them in New Eden Time."

"Hum. I see." Admiral Noah pulled thoughtfully at his beard. "Three-points are really quite tame. You must have provoked the animals."

Both young men shook their heads. "We didn't do nothin'," Lester said.

"By Cain you didn't." Admiral Noah gave the two a narrow look and shook his head. "I haven't got the time now to figure out what you two are up to, but I will later."

Adam set the sack of apples on the table. "Show me the picture, Admiral Noah. We have to hurry."

"Right. Come with me." He started down the long hallway.

Shem, Japheth, and Ham looked at each other. "Picture?" Shem asked.

Japheth and Ham shrugged. Overcome with curiosity, the three sons hurried after their father.

Chapter 14

LESTER WATCHED THEM UNTIL THEY'D MARCHED ALL the way down the long hallway and turned into a room at the far end. An evil smile crawled across his face as his view came back to the unguarded sack of apples on the table. He nudged his partner in crime.

"Huh? W-what?"

"Shusss." Lester glanced at the woman by the counter. Majiah, Ham's wife, hummed a happy tune as she shredded a head of cabbage on a long, shinny grater. Mrs. Noah and Desmorah stepped out of a back room, carrying laundry baskets, and strolled out of the common room. Lester listened to their footsteps get softer and softer, and then fade altogether.

"Now's our chance," he said inching closer to the table.

"I'm hungry," Lester complained, watching Majiah preparing the evening meal.

"You're always hungry. Let's steal those apples and give them to the Evols. We'll get our reward and then get out of here."

"B-but Lester-"

"You can eat when we get home."

"B-but-"

"Shussh, bonehead. She'll hear you." Lester glanced nervously at Majiah, but she hadn't heard. He quietly pulled the sack off the table and backed tiptoed out of the common room. Once out of sight, he started running. Down the long ramp flew, past the pen of large animals, back, back through the immense boat toward the dark storage area."

"But Lester," Castor called as he tried to keep up.

They had plunged deep inside the dark belly of the huge ship before Lester stopped and turned back angrily at Castor. "BUT WHAT!"

Castor thumped to a halt, breathing hard and bent over trying to catch his breath. "Y-you said we're going to get out of here. H-how do we get out of here?"

"Bonehead! We'll use the Dream Doodler."

"B-but we don't have the Dream Doodler. That Adam Beam kid has it."

Lester opened his mouth to call him something nasty, when he realized Castor was right. He stood there a long moment, his jaw hanging. He always hated it when Castor was right about anything. "Well . . . well . . . well I'll just have to think of some other way," he said, pretending that there might actually be some other way off Noah's Ark, but of course there wasn't.

With spider's feet crawling up their spines, the two ne'er-do-wells crept further into the darkness. "Hello," Lester squeaked weakly. "Hello Mr. Evols. Are you here?"

Behind him, Castor gave a yelp. Lester turned with a jolt. His partner in crime stood stiff as a statue, his face white as a Lighton's shirt, and his eyes wider than baseballs. He was trying to say something, but all that came out of his mouth were unintelligible babbles.

"What!" Lester squeaked.

Castor raised a shaking finger at the three sets of eyes that floated in the darkness nearby. Castor gulped and held out the sack of apples. "I brought them. See? Just like I said I would."

"Very good, human," a high scratchy voice said. Castor couldn't tell which of the Evols has spoken. Even though they were close now, their dark hoods hid their faces. He gulped again. That is, if they even had faces. The hems of the robes floated above the floor.

"His Magnificence will be pleased," a different voice said and a bony hand extended from the sleeve of one of the dark robes. "Give them to me."

Castor started to hand the sack over, but stopped. "What about my reward."

"Having served His Magnificence is reward enough for you, human."

In spite of being nearly frightened out of his skin, Lester wasn't going to give in so easily. "I-I said I wanted gold . . . and a way back to New Eden," he added.

Another voice spoke then, deep, resonant, so unlike the Evol's squeaky voices. "Why would you want to return to *that* place when I can give you all that you desire here?"

Lester and Castor spun in the direction the voice had come. Far down a dark valley between stacks and mounds of boxes and barrels, a bright light appeared; the strangest light either of the young thieves had ever seen. It was a golden color, sort of like the glow of a Lighton, except that it didn't fill the room like a Lighton's light did. The mounds on either side of him remained as dark as ever as he passed them by. The only thing the light illuminated was the tall man walking toward them; encircling his whole being like a golden halo.

As the man came closer, Lester was struck by his proud bearing, his fine clothes. Lester and Castor were almost mesmerized by his handsome features, but there was something strange about his eyes.

The Evols bowed as the man approached. "Your Magnificence," they said.

One of them said, "He has brought the apples but won't give them to us. He wants a reward." The Evol chuckled. "Foolish human that he is."

The man merely smiled. His very being radiated a strange energy, dark and malevolent, that the two thieves felt down to their bones. "We are not above rewarding those who serve us." The man turned. "What is it you two seek?"

"Gold," Lester blurted, hi knees shaking, his teeth chattering.

The man laughed. "You ask for mere gold? Do you not know who I am? That I can give you your heart's desires? Fame, wealth, power beyond your wildest imagination. If you will but bow down to me, these all can be yours."

Lester wasn't sure what he meant by that, but something about the offer and this man made him all squirmy inside. He cast a questioning look at his partner. Castor's attention was frozen upon the man inside the aura of light, and his head slowly shook back and forth, as if rejecting the offer.

Lester's chest grew suddenly tight.

"Your Magnificence," an Evol said, "These two are not of this time. They come from New Eden Time."

The man in the golden light gave a shudder at the mention of New Eden. "I know. No matter. They are here now, and in this age I can give riches and kingdoms to whomever I wish. This world has been given over to me and I can do with it as I please."

Lester stammered. "I-I don't think I need no kingdoms. Really." What was he thinking, rejecting such a wonderful offer? The tightness in his chest made his breathing come in quick, short pants. He didn't understand his growing panic. Something about this man terrified him.

"You reject my offer?" The man roared, the golden aura of light surrounding him taking on a reddish hue.

"I only wanted a little gold," Lester squeaked, taking a step backward.

"You'll get nothing, foolish human. I have no time for humoring weak mortals. GIVE ME THE APPLES!" The man's eyes became bright orbs like burning coals.

Castor gave a shriek of fright, spun on his heels and fled in terror back up the aisle the way they'd come. Lester turned to run too, but he tripped in the darkness and crashed to the floor. In an instant the Evols surrounded him.

The man came closer, the ball of light that enveloped him burning bright and pulsing with red anger. "You shall know the consequences of rejecting me, *human*."

* * *

IN THE LIBRARY ROOM, Admiral Noah searched the tall bookshelves where hundred of volumes stood side-by-side in neat rows. Their spines and covers were green and blue, red and black. Some had no covers at all, only loose sheets of papers held together with stout, golden clips. Adam Beam thought it would be fun to explore this vast collection of books, which contained the knowledge of the First Time. All that knowledge would have been lost in the Flood if Admiral Noah hadn't collected these books and protected them aboard his great ship.

"Ah, here it is." Admiral Noah pulled a tall book from a middle shelf and opened it upon the library table. The book was filled with beautiful pictures. Most of the pictures were of a neatly groomed garden. Some showed winding paths through beds of bright flowers. Others showed waterfalls, crowned with colorful rainbows.

The pictures were vibrant and so real-looking that Adam imagined he could reach into them and touch the leaves or feel the waters. They weren't anything like the old-fashion photograph in the Before Time books on display in the Gloraiana History Museum. They were more like the holographic images that appeared in the Exploretime *Wonders of Creation* Cube.

Admiral Noah pointed to one of them. "This is a picture of the Healing Tree."

Adam said, "That looks like the tree that grows along the Golden Avenue in Glorainia."

"It is the same," Zonia said. "Now I know it really can help Gracy. We can just go to Glorainia and pick some."

Adam thought about that. "I don't know, Zonia.

Dad told me that in New Eden Time, those leaves are for the healing of the nations."

"Hum. Maybe you're right."

Adam said to Noah, "This picture is just what I need. Now all I have to do is imagine you standing right next to that tree and then Zonia, Toby, and I will join you there through the Dream Draw Portal."

"I'm excited to be going back to the Garden one more time," Admiral Noah said.

"You've been there before?" Zonia asked.

He nodded, a faraway look on his face. "It's a long story."

But he didn't have time to tell them the story for at that moment a horrible shriek — a sound of sheer terror, muffled by the heavy floor timbers — came from the deck below.

"What was that?" Zonia cried.

Shem said, "It came from the storage hold."

Ham said, "Those two villains again. What trouble have they gotten into now?"

"Let's find out." Admiral Noah rushed out the door. Instead of returning to the common room, he took off in another direction, along a dark hallway and down a flight of stairs. It was a shortcut to the storage area directly below the family's living quarters.

For a man six hundred years old, Admiral Noah was quick on his feet. He dashed down the steps as if he were only two hundred. As he reached the floor of the storage deck, he flipped a switch mounted on a thick post and the whole place lit up. All the mounds of supplies came sharply into view, and so did the strange creatures that floated above Lester Groutt. Lester was curled up into a ball on the floor. Nearby stood a tall man within a halo of reddish light.

Adam reached the floor right behind Admiral Noah. "Those are Evols," he said. He'd seen them before in the cave where he, Zonia, Enoch, and Toby had rescued the apples the Evols had stolen from Grandfather Adam. "That's the man they call His Magnificence."

The man in the halo of red light turned and looked at Admiral Noah.

"Do not involve yourself in my affairs, human," he said to Admiral Noah.

"I know who you are. You are not wanted here. I order you to leave my ship at once."

Zonia came down the stairs next with Toby, and then Ham, Shem, and Japheth. She nudged Adam and pointed at Lester Groutt. "There are the apples."

The sack lay on the floor next to the thief, close to His Magnificence, the evil ruler of the Evols.

Adam whispered, "Come with me." They darted behind a tall mound covered in a shiny gray tarpaulin.

Zonia said, "You have a plan. I can always tell."

"While   Noah   keeps   His   Magnificence

distracted, we'll sneak in behind him and grab the sack of Adam's Apples."

"How will we get past him and the Evols?"

"With this." Adam took the Dream Doodler from its holster.

Zonia looked puzzled, and then grinned. "The Disappear Dazzler button!" She almost clapped for joy, but remembered to be quiet.

An evil, mocking laugh reached them from the other side of the mound. "You think you know me. If you really did, you'd fall to your knees trembling."

"It is you who will fall to your knees, but not before me, but before the Creator of All."

His Magnificence gave a sudden snake-like hiss. "Do not use that name in my presence, human!"

Adam whispered, "You ready?"

Zonia nodded and grabbed a fistful of Toby's orange fur in one hand and took Adam's hand in the other. For the Disappear Dazzler to work, everyone had to hold onto each other.

"Here goes." Adam pressed the button on the Dream Doodler. Of course, nothing at all appeared to have happened to Adam, Zonia, and Toby because when you disappear-dazzle you can still see each other. If, however, you'd been observing the three of them from afar, you'd have been startled to have seen them blink out of sight in the wink of an eye.

Creeping quietly around the mound, they

tiptoed toward the evil being. Neither His Magnificence nor the Evols saw the children and their pet tiger.

Admiral Noah, in the meantime, advanced on the man in the reddish halo now glowing with the angry color of blood. "You don't like hearing the name Creator of All, do you?"

His Magnificence hissed again and took a step backward. Adam saw that the name really did frighten him.

"I'll take my leave of you, human. The apples will come with me." His Magnificence reached for the sack on the floor.

At that moment the sack leaped from the ground under its own power and floated momentarily in the air. The next moment the sack flew speedily away. It swooped past the animal pens, and up the long ramp that led to the top deck of the Ark.

The sight startled them all, and then Admiral Noah gave a laugh. "It would appear that The Creator of All has a different plan for the apples."

His Magnificence hissed like a snake and put his hands in front of his face as if to protect himself from that Name. "I don't know how you performed that trickery, human," the evil being of light snarled, "but you haven't seen the last of me."

Admiral Noah said, "On this ship we worship the Creator of All, and even now He is present with us."

With wide fear in his eyes, the evil being looked all around. His Evol henchmen shuddered too, and began fading from sight.

"There will come a time when you won't expect me. When that time comes, there I will be, waiting for you." The halo of light began to shrink. When it was only a speck of light, it winked out completely.

Shem, Ham, and Japheth gathered around their father. "We must be vigilant, pop," Shem said.

Admiral Noah nodded. "Yes, my son, but so long as we are inside this ship, that serpent of old cannot harm us." Admiral Noah helped Lester to his feet. The young man was trembling; his face was white as a lily.

Ham said to his father, "How did you make those apples float away like that?"

"I didn't do it." He looked around, "I suspect those children from New Eden Time had a hand in it. They were here a moment ago, but now they're gone. If I haven't missed my guess, we'll find them upstairs waiting for us. And they will have the apples with them."

Chapter 15

ADAM, ZONIA, AND TOBY DIDN'T STOP RUNNING until they skidded to a halt inside the large common room. When they did, they discovered Castor Groutt trembling in the corner and staring at the doorway. The women were there too, staring right at Adam as if Mrs. Noah and her daughters-in-law could see them, but then he realized what held their attention. It was the sack of apples he was holding. To the women it must have appeared to be floating in the air.

Adam grinned and pressed the Disappear Dazzler button on the Dream Doodler. The two children and a huge orange tiger popped into view right before their eyes.

Majiah dropped a pan.

Desmorah gasped.

Castor shrieked and covered his head.

"It's only us," Zonia said. "Don't be afraid."

"How did you do that?" Mrs. Noah asked.

"With this." Adam held up the Dream Doodler, and then put it back in its holster.

Zonia said to Castor, "Are you all right?"

He shook his head. "T-the Evols and that hor-horrible man in the golden light are very bad people."

"Yes they are," Adam said, "but if you trust the Great King, those evil beings can't hurt you."

"I-I don't never want to see those - those scary *things* again!" Castor trembled so badly he could hardly speak. "I-I want to trust. I-I just don't know how."

Zonia said, "It's easy. All you have to do is ask the Great King to live inside you. When you do, He will, and neither Evols nor the one they call 'His Magnificence', can hurt you."

Castor said, "I do trust in the Great King."

"Wonderful!" Zonia said. "If you truly mean it, you have nothing more to fear from those evil creatures."

Castor slowly stopped trembling. He even managed a small smile. "I think it worked. What do I do now?"

Adam said, "You've already done all that you have to do. From now on just do your best to obey the Great King's rules, and if you sometimes forget and don't, then tell Him your sorry and ask Him to forgive you. He always will."

"That's all? T-that isn't too hard."

"It's simple," Zonia said.

Approaching footsteps sounded outside the doorway, and Admiral Noah, Seth, Ham, and Japheth strode into the common room. Lester Groutt was with them, looking pale and kind of shaky on his feet. Shem held onto Lester's arm as if helping him to stand. Adam figured that Lester was suffering from a severe case of fright!

Admiral Noah gave hearty laugh. "What did I tell you, boys? There is Adam, Zonia, and Toby, and the sack of apples too."

Shem helped Lester into a chair by the table.

Adam said, "Now let's hurry get the healing leaves so that we can make Gracy better."

"I'm ready!" Admiral Noah said, his eyes gleaming in anticipation of seeing the Garden one last time. He said to his sons, "You keep an eye on these two while we're gone. They've caused enough trouble for us already."

"I-I won't cause you no more trouble," Castor said.

Lester scowled at his friend, but said not a word because his heart still pounded hard inside his chest.

"Okay, I'll just imagine you standing by the tree," Adam said. "Ready?"

"Ready," Admiral Noah said.

"Toby and I are ready too," Zonia said.

"Okay, let's go." Adam thought about the tree he'd seen in the picture book, and imagined Admiral Noah standing right next to it. He closed his eyes and waved the Dream Doodler in the air and pressed the Dream Draw button.

But when he opened his eyes, there wasn't a Dream Door portal. And Admiral Noah was still standing there right in front of him.

Adam looked at the Dream Doodler. "It didn't work."

"Try it again," Zonia urged.

"All right." Adam closed his eyes and imagined Mr. Noah standing right next to the Tree of Life in the middle of the Garden of Eden. He waved the Dream Doodler and pressed the button.

Nothing happened. The common room remained exactly as it had been a moment before. But no. Now in the middle of the room a glittering point of light appeared. The light grew larger and brighter until it filled the room.

"It's Zekor," Adam said as the giant Lighton appeared in the middle of the light. Unlike His Magnificence, whose halo of light that only showed on himself, Zekor's brilliant halo lit up the whole room even to the corners, and shown warmly upon each of them.

"Hi Zekor," Zonia said and ran to the Lighton, giving him a big hug. Zekor took her up into his strong arms and gave her a gentle hug back.

Adam said, "The Dream Doodler didn't work. Why didn't it work?"

Toby rubbed against Zekor's leg and the Lighton reached down with one hand and petted the big Siberian Tiger. "It didn't work because there are still some places where the children of Adam cannot go. Except for only a very few people, the Garden of the Great King is still off limits."

Admiral Noah and his family stared at the giant Lighton. None of them seemed able to speak yet.

Admiral Noah was the first to find his tongue. "How will we heal Gracy? She did a great service for the Creator of All, the Great King, as you refer to Him."

"The Great King is well aware of Gracy's service, and of her urgent needs. He sent me to give you these." Zekor's arm swept a small circle; glittering light sparkling off his sleeves. His hand opened and upon his palm was a single green leaf. "This is from the Tree that grows on either side of river that flows from beneath the Great King's throne. He sent it to you, to heal Gracy."

Noah took the leaf in both hands like a priceless jewel. "Thank you, Zekor. This is a wonderful gift indeed." He turned to Adam. "Use your amazing Dream Doodler to take us back to Gracy and Kitah. They must be wondering where we've been."

"What about Lester and Castor?" Adam asked? "We can't leave them here."

Zekor nodded. "I will take them back to Gloriania with me. The Great King wishes to speak to them." He looked at Castor. "In particular He wishes to honor you, Mr. Groutt."

"M-me?" Castor stammered.

"Him!" Lester scoffed. "Why would the Great King want to honor *him?* What about me?"

Zekor smiled. "You, Mr. Mudd, have not yet invited the Great King into your heart."

Lester's mouth unhinged. "And the bonehead did?"

"I-I did, Lester. I don't ever want to see those evil beings again. Now the Great King will protect me. H-he'll protect you too, if you want him to."

Lester shivered. "Seeing those Evols with my own two eyes, I don't want to again either. That one they call 'His Magnificence', he made me feel all squirmy inside."

Zekor said, "That's a good sign, Mr. Mudd. It shows that you haven't given yourself over to his powers. He desires to have you, you know. He has claimed ownership over a great many children of Adam. You definitely do not want to be counted among them."

Lester shook his head. "No, I don't."

Zekor nodded. "Think about it, young man, and then make your decision. Now, you two need to return to Glorainia with me."

Adam said, "How will they get back? Don't you need the Dream Doodler to do it?"

"We will return by the Wind Way."

"The Wind Way goes through Admiral Noah's time too?" Zonia asked. She had only ever used it to travel around New Eden.

"The Wind Way goes where the Great King

commands it to go. And right at this moment, He has commanded it to go right through the middle of Noah's Ark." As Zekor spoke, the familiar swishing sound of the Wind Way began to stir the air. Zekor stepped between Lester and Castor and put a huge hand upon each of their shoulders. Zekor gave Adam and Zonia a final smile, and a wink sent Toby's way. "I will see you three shortly," The giant Lighton said as the sound grew louder. It seemed to swallow up the three of them and in a shower of emerald light they disappeared.

"My word," Mrs. Noah said. "People of the future do come and go in the strangest ways."

"We need to go too," Zonia said urgently. "Gracy needs those healing leaves right away."

"Absolutely," Admiral Noah said in a commanding tone, resuming his role as admiral of his sea creature navy. "Mr. Adam, transport us at once back to Gracy's side."

"Aye-aye," Adam said. He gave a proper salute, and then closed his eyes, imagining Admiral Noah once again beneath the crystal dome on the sea floor. He imagined Kitah and Gracy and the little EFTS submarine exactly as he'd left them. Waving the Dream Doodler in the air, he pressed the Dream Draw button. In a wink Admiral Noah disappeared and a Dream Door portal opened in the air right next to the big table there in the common room.

"Let's go!" Zonia said. She leaped through the

Dream Door with Adam and Toby right on her heals.

Plop! Plop! Plop! They landed on the muddy seafloor and sank to their ankles in the sticky goop.

"Ugh," Zonia said, making a disgusted face. "I forgot about the mud."

Toby snarled, lifted one paw and shook it, and then the other, but it did little good.

"Yeah, I forgot too," Adam said.

"What took you so long?" Admiral Noah joked, and then his view went to Gracy and his expression became serious. "Gracy doesn't look good at all. Her skin is red and swollen."

Kitah was still kneeling at brave dolphin's side. She looked up at them and said, "Gracy needs to get back into the water soon. She's very weak and is having trouble breathing."

"We brought the healing leaves," Zonia said. She wanted to sound hopeful, but the sight Gracy's blistered skin and the sound of her weak breath through the blowhole on top of her head filled Zonia with sadness.

Admiral Noah knelt it the mud next to Gracy. "You must eat this leaf. It will make you better."

Gracy only looked at the healing leaf in his hand. She had no strength to even open her mouth.

Zonia said, "Gracy, please eat it."

She made a faint sound that none of them understood.

Kitah said worriedly, "She can't eat."

"But she must," Adam said, falling to his knees beside the sick dolphin. "She was so brave. The Great King sent the leaf so that she would get better."

"Then it must be The Great King's will that Gracy gets better," Admiral Noah said.

Adam said, "The Bible says we ought to pray that the Great King's will be done."

"What's a bible?" Kitah asked.

"It's the book that the Great King had many different men write to show mankind how to live, and how to be saved." Adam thought a moment. "It was written long after the flood. That's why you haven't heard about it."

Admiral Noah nodded. "It makes sense that the Creator of All would give mankind a rule book to live by. He had Grandfather Adam write a book, and Grandfather Enoch too. I have copies of them aboard this ship."

"Let's ask the Great King right now," Adam said.

Kitah's worried expression brightened a bit. "That's a great idea!"

They all joined hands around Gracy. Even Toby lent his paws. Adam said, "Great King, we know it's your will that Gracy gets better. If it wasn't, You wouldn't have sent the healing leaf from the tree that grows in Your Kingdom. But Gracy is too weak now to eat it. Please give Gracy the strength she needs to eat the healing leaf so that she can get better."

When Adam finished the prayer, Admiral Noah put the leaf close to Gracy's mouth. The brave dolphin's eyes followed his hand. At first she just stared at the leaf, and then she gave a little dolphin-chirp. Her big brown eyes appeared more alert.

Zonia said, "Oh, please eat the leaf, Gracy."

Gracy turned her large eyes toward her. Zonia wanted to give the dolphin a gentle pet, but her skin looked so painfully red and blistered that she was afraid she'd hurt Gracy even more.

"You can do it," Adam urged.

Admiral Noah said, "Just take a little bite."

Gracy opened her mouth and Admiral Noah helped her get an edge of the leaf between her teeth. Gracy bit down on it and a glint of golden light began to glow around her long, bottle-shaped nose. It seemed to strengthen the sick dolphin a little. Gracy took another bite from the leaf and this time managed to swallow.

The golden aura brightened and started to swirl like hundreds of tiny golden ice crystals in a cold winter morning's air. This light wasn't cold though. Adam felt its gentle warmth radiating out from Gracy. It was the same gentle warmth he remembered feeling when he'd stood in the presence of the Great King.

Glittering brighter now, the golden light moved along her blistered body, up onto her fins, and then spread wide at her broad tail, surrounding Gracy is a splendid glow.

Admiral Noah gasped. The ugly red scaring was becoming smooth bluish dolphin skin.

"It's working," Kitah said, her eyes round with wonder.

Toby walked around the dolphin and made a mewing noise, sniffing the air as he went.

Zonia clapped her hands and looked excitedly at her big brother. "Gracy is going to be all right!"

As if in answer, Gracy began chattering, as if talking to them, but all they heard was dolphin squeaks, no words that any of them could make out.

"How come we can't understand her now?" Zonia asked Adam.

Admiral Noah stood, his knees and hands muddy. He didn't seem to notice. "We can't understand her because she's out of the water. Her voice sounds different when she's underwater where The Creator of All designed her to live."

Adam said, "You're right. Gracy needs to return to the sea. Quickly, everyone back into the EFTS. You too Toby. Dolphins are designed to live in the water, not Siberian Tigers."

They all returned to the little submarine except Adam who remained at Gracy's side. Once everyone was safely aboard, Adam stroked Gracy's sleak intelligent head. "I'm going to Dream Draw you back into the sea where you belong. Do you understand me?"

Gracy gave several long, excited chirps. Although Adam didn't understand her words, he knew that she had understood him and that she was excited to be back in the sea with her friends and family.

Adam said, "You did a wonderful thing, rescuing those apples. The Great King will never forget. Maybe someday in New Eden Time, we will meet again?"

Another long series of chirps told him that Gracy hoped so too.

Adam stood and slogged his way through the mud back to the submarine, and climbed the ladder. Before descending down the hatch, he looked back at Gracy laying on the muddy seafloor. How much happier she was going to be once back in the water, where she belonged.

With a sudden smile springing to his lips, he shut the hatch and turned the locking wheel tight.

Chapter 16

ADAM BEAM WALKED TO THE FRONT OF THE submarine and turned. Admiral Noah, Kitah, Zonia, and Toby were looking at him as if to say, *Well, what now?*

He was wondering the same thing. "This might be complicated. I suppose I could try to do it all at once, or one at a time." He looked at the Dream Doodler and scrunched his lips to one side, thinking about it.

"What seems to be the problem," Admiral Noah asked.

"Well, I have to Dream Doodle a Dream Door with Gracy already in it, swimming free in the ocean. But we can't go into it ourselves because we aren't dolphins."

"Of course we aren't," Zonia said, and Toby gave a tiger snarl in agreement.

"So," Adam continued, "We will let the Dream

Door portal close, like it always does. And then, I have to dream draw a second portal, only this time I have to imagine Admiral Noah and Kitah back in the Ark, standing beside the big table, just the way you were when you two left."

"But we can go through *that* dream door, Adam," Zonia pointed out.

"Yes, we can . . . only, what will happen to this submarine?"

"I suppose it will just sit here on the bottom of the sea forever," Zonia said.

"Or maybe it will simply vanish once it's no longer needed," Kitah suggested.

"Does it matter?" Admiral Noah asked.

Adam thought a moment. "I don't know if it matters or not. What if someone finds it after the flood waters go away? What happens if it is found a thousand years from now?"

Admiral Noah chuckled. "That will be a big puzzle for them to figure out." He got serious then. "I wouldn't worry too much about that. The way the earth is being broken up and shifted around, this little underwater boat of yours will be buried so deep in mud and silt, it will never be found."

That made sense. "Okay, I won't worry about it. Now that that's settled, let's get started."

Adam closed his eyes and imagined Gracy back in the sea, swimming with her friends. He waved the Dream Doodler and pressed the Dream Draw button, and right there in front of them a dream door portal opened up. They all leaned closer for a good look. Gracy was once again swimming happily with her friends. She looked back as if able to see them through the Dream Door portal. And then her voice came over the speakers.

"Thank you for taking care of me and putting me back where I belong! I enjoyed meeting all of you!" And as she swam away, her voice changed until all that could be heard over the underwater speakers was happy dolphin chattering.

The portal closed.

Kitah sighed. "Gracy was wonderful," she said, and everyone agreed.

Adam said, "It's time we all go back to where we belong too."

"Very good idea, young Adam Beam. And then I can stop being Admiral Noah and just be plain old Noah. I think I like that better."

They laughed, and in the time it took for Adam to think about it and wave the Dream Doodler, they were standing in the common room, back aboard the Ark.

* * *

IT WAS a little sad to have to say goodbye to Noah and his family, but Adam, Zonia, and Toby were very anxious go back to New Eden Time and their lovely home in the city of Glorainia where the Great King's rule filled the whole land with peace.

They missed Mom and Dad too.

Before they left, Mrs. Noah and her daughters-in-law gave Adam and Zonia goodbye-hugs, and Mr. Noah and his three sons shook their hands.

"I'm really looking forward to seeing New Eden someday," Noah said.

Adam said, "You will like it. We'll all see each other again someday."

Shem said, "That's a wonderfully encouraging thought." He sighed. "But for the near future, we are going to have a tough time of it when we leave this ship."

Japheth nodded. "It will be hard work in the beginning, but we've brought tools, machines, and a huge library of books to help us build a new civilization."

"Building is what I enjoy doing the most," Ham said with a faraway look in his eyes as if he was already planning cities and roads and towers.

Zonia said, "The next time I hear someone talk about Noah's Ark, I'll never think of it the same way I used to."

"How is our ship different from what you imagined?" Noah asked, smiling.

She shrugged. "I guess I thought it was just a big boat, and that it probably smelled like a barn. I had no idea the Ark was so complicated, and it doesn't hardly smell at all, thanks to Ham's clever devices."

Ham grinned and a blush came to his face.

And then it really was time to leave. Adam took the sack of apples and Zonia put on her backpack.

"Ready?" he asked.

"I'm more than ready," Zonia said.

Adam thought about their home, about their cozy house and mom and dad. With a wave of the Dream Doodler, that very picture of happiness and love appeared suspended in the air.

"Goodbye goodbye," Adam and Zonia called and Toby gave an excited roar. The three of them leaped through the dream door portal and their feet . . . and paws . . . thumped upon the floor of their very own kitchen.

"You're home already?" Molly Beam exclaimed. She looked surprised and excited all at the same time. To Mrs. Beam, they had only been away a few minutes.

Adam and Zonia ran to her wide arms. Bud Beam joined in on the big group hug. "I'm glad to be home," Zonia said, giving her mom another hug. "We were away so long, and so much happened. Did you know that Noah's Ark doesn't smell?"

Bud and Molly Beam laughed. "I didn't know that," her father said.

Adam said, "It's amazing. The Ark is bigger than the block we live on, and it's filled with books and machines and all kinds of tools."

Toby gave a snarl, nudging Adam with his nose. Adam laughed. "Yes, and animals too. I didn't forget Toby."

Dad said, "I see that you've recovered the Apples that those two thieves stole. The Great King will be so pleased. Soon you can begin planting their seed throughout Glorainia, and then New Eden. You know, every year the world becomes more and more like the Garden of Eden once was. I can hardly remember what the Before Time was like anymore."

Mom said, "I'm sure you have so much to tell us. It sounds like you three had a very interesting Dream Door Adventure."

Zonia said, "We did, and we do have a lot to tell you." She was about to describe the common room with the big table where Noah and his family ate meals when from the direction of the Great King's palace, beautiful bells began ringing.

Dad looked at his wife. "Sounds like yet another soul has invited the Great King into their heart."

They went to the window to watch the glow of light above the far palace. It looked like a soft rainbow, and the colors seemed to dance in the air.

"I wonder who it was." Mom said. "I can't wait until the Lightons announce their name."

But Adam knew, and so did Zonia.

Castor had made the right choice aboard the Ark. And now Lester had too.

About Douglas Hirt

Douglas Hirt was born in Illinois, but heeding Horace Greeley's admonition to "Go west, young man", he headed to New Mexico at eighteen. Doug earned a Bachelor's degree from the College of Santa Fe and a Masters of Science degree from Eastern New Mexico University. During this time he spent several summers living in a tent in the desert near Carlsbad, New Mexico, conducting biological baseline surveys for the Department of Energy.

Doug drew heavily from this "desert life" when writing his first novel, DEVIL'S WIND. In 1991 Doug's novel, A PASSAGE OF SEASONS, won the Colorado Authors' League Top Hand Award. His 1998 book, BRANDISH, and 1999 DEAD-WOOD, were finalists for the SPUR award given by the Western Writers of America.

A short story writer, and the author of twenty-nine novels and one book of non fiction, Doug now makes his home in Colorado Springs with his wife Kathy and their two children, Rebecca and Derick. When not writing or traveling to research his novels,

Doug enjoys collecting and restoring old English sports cars.

About Terry James

Terry James is author, general editor, and co-author of numerous books on Bible prophecy, hundreds of thousands of which have been sold worldwide. James is a frequent lecturer on the study of end time phenomena, and interviews often with national and international media on topics involving world issues and events as they might relate to Bible prophecy.

He has appeared in major documentaries and media forums, in all media formats, in America, Europe, and Asia.

He appeared in the History Channel series, The Nostradamus Effect.

He is an active member of the PreTrib Research Center Study Group, a prophecy research think-tank founded by Dr. Tim LaHaye, the co-author of the multi-million selling "Left Behind" series of novels. He is a regular participant in the annual Tulsa mid-America prophecy conference, where he speaks, and holds a Question and Answer series of sessions on current world events as they might relate to Bible prophecy.

Terry James has been blind since 1993 due to a

degenerative retinal disease (retinitis pigmentosa). He uses the Jobs Accessible Word System (JAWS) – which is voice synthesis—to write and conduct business over the Internet.

His former profession was in public relations, advertising, marketing, and publicity and promotion.

He received his education from Arkansas Polytechnic Institute, Memphis Academy of Arts, and University of Arkansas at Little Rock.

He served in both corporate and government positions for 25 years, before becoming a full-time writer.

James also served in the United States Air Force from October 1966 through October 1970.) He served at Randolph AFB, Texas, in the T-38 section, a mission dedicated to training pilots in high-performance jet fighter-trainers.

Terry James and his wife, Margaret, live near Little Rock, Arkansas.

www.ingramcontent.com/pod-product-compliance
Lightning Source LLC
Chambersburg PA
CBHW020911180626

46816CB00007BA/2356